四期

SINO-AMERICAN JOURNAL *Of* COMPARATIVE LITERATURE

中美比较文学

主编 张 华
Paul Allen Miller

中国社会科学出版社

图书在版编目（CIP）数据

中美比较文学．第四期：英文/张华，（美）保罗·艾伦·米勒（Paul Allen Miller）主编．—北京：中国社会科学出版社，2020.10

ISBN 978-7-5203-6709-7

Ⅰ．①中… Ⅱ．①张…②保… Ⅲ．①比较文学—文学研究—中国、美国—英文 Ⅳ．①I206 ②I712.06

中国版本图书馆 CIP 数据核字（2020）第 115048 号

出 版 人 赵剑英
责任编辑 夏 侠
责任校对 胡国秀
责任印制 张雪娇

出 版 中国社会科学出版社
社 址 北京鼓楼西大街甲 158 号
邮 编 100720
网 址 http://www.csspw.cn
发 行 部 010-84083685
门 市 部 010-84029450
经 销 新华书店及其他书店

印 刷 北京君升印刷有限公司
装 订 廊坊市广阳区广增装订厂
版 次 2020 年 10 月第 1 版
印 次 2020 年 10 月第 1 次印刷

开 本 710×1000 1/16
印 张 10
插 页 2
字 数 150 千字
定 价 68.00 元

《中美比较文学》（*Sino-American Journal of Comparative Literature*）为北京语言大学创办，并由比较文学界同仁共同编辑。中外学者的来稿由编委会负责审阅，该连续性出版物将由中国社会科学出版社出版，中英文双语发行。

该连续性出版物旨在集中展示比较文学界在比较文学与世界文学学科范围内及相关学科的最新研究成果，探讨前沿理论问题，拓展文学批评空间，研究学术焦点现象，以促进比较文学与世界文学研究领域的最平等、最直接、最充分的学术交流。

Sino-American Journal of Comparative Literature is founded by Beijing Language and Culture University. The journal is published by the China

Social Sciences Press both in English and in Chinese. The founder and editors, as well as the members of the editorial board, as experts in the field of comparative literature are responsible for refereeing all submissions. Articles submitted in Chinese and in English are edited by the editorial board.

The journal is designed to be a platform to gather and exhibit the latest research findings in Comparative Literature, World Literature and related disciplines. Its mission is to explore the latest theoretical issues in both countries and to expand the range of literary criticism available in each. It aims to promote a full and critical dialogue in the field of Comparative Literature and World Literature as well as intercultural comprehension.

RAPAPORT, Herman (Wake Forest University)
SHANKMAN, Steven (University of Oregon)
ZALLOUA, Zahi (Whitman College)

目　录

Say No to Fungibility! Resisting Neoliberalism in the Name of the Universal-Particular …… Paul Allen Miller(1)

World Literature and the Promise of Digital Publishing …… Jeffrey R. Di Leo(20)

The Maze and the Matrix: Fantasizing the Missing Other …… Jacob Blevins(36)

Ironic Enchantment and Postcolonial Futures …… Nicole Simek(56)

Unification, Fit-in, and Diaspora: An Ecocritical Analysis of Representation of the Position of Humanity in Chinese Literature …… SONG Lili(93)

From Shanghai Beauty to Earth Mother: The Retreat of Sexuality and the Rise of Productivity in Wang Anyi's Writings …… CHEN Dandan(123)

Say No to Fungibility! Resisting Neoliberalism in the Name of the Universal-Particular

Paul Allen Miller *

中文摘要 本文首先回顾了马克思对于商品以及作为一般等价物的货币的定义。进而提出：在商品化和数字化的世界中必须坚持普遍的特殊性，这就是说：个体的经验不可缩减，但同时又需要将这种经验转化成他人可辨识的形式以便与他人共同形成有意义的行动。讨论这种理论困境之后，本文讨论了三个抵抗缩减替代性的例子：杜拉斯小说《塔尔奎尼亚的小马》中的荒诞感，作为一种精神实践形式的禅宗公案以及苏格拉底对悖论探求。最后本文探讨了亚里士多德在《诗学》中的观点，他指出诗比历史更具哲理性的原因就在于诗虽然着眼于普遍性，但同时处理的都是特殊经验。

关键词 商品；可替代性；马克思；禅宗；苏格拉底；普遍性；特殊性

Abstract This paper begins with a reading of Marx's definition

---

* 作者为美国南卡罗莱纳大学比较文学教授，《中美比较文学》外方主编。研究方向为古典学、比较文学。

of the commodity and of money as the universal equivalent. It argues that the world of commodification and digitality must be resisted on multiple fronts, but above all by insisting on the universal particular, that is to say, on both the irreducibility of our experience and the simultaneous need to translate that experience into terms capable of being recognized by others and able to organize others for meaningful action. After this theoretical preliminary, it looks at three examples of resistance to reductive fungibility: the absurd in Duras's Les petits chevaux de Tarquinia, Zen Koans as a spiritual practice, and the Socratic pursuit of aporia. The paper will close with a meditation on Aristotle's claim in the Poetics that poetry is more philosophical than history because poetry is both addressed to the universal and deals only in the particular.

Keywords commodity, fungibility, Marx, Zen, Socrates, universal, particular.

The first premise of knowledge in the culture of neoliberalism is digitality: the ability to represent all significant qualia in numerical terms, and therefore the infinite reproducibility of those same qualia. The unique, the local, the unrepeatable, is by definition from this perspective ephemeral, lacking in significance, and in all likelihood illusory. It is not "evidence based", not "testable". This premise of digitality and reproducibility is what guarantees the rationality of our scientific, economic, and political enterprises in the neoliberal universe, a set of qualities that posits an epistemic ontology in which objects are only knowable to the extent they are subject to calculation. Truly meaningful experience should be reducible to a universal measure. Neoliberalism is, in this sense, profoundly Platonist.

In the neoliberal university, therefore, we need to be able to show the value added of every class and to quantify that addition in uniform terms. What cannot be measured does not exist. The neoliberal university accordingly has as its ideal the perfect fungibility of knowledge and experience. From teaching evaluations, to assessment, to value added, biochemistry and romantic poetry should be quantifiable in comparable if not identical ways and a rubric produced in which each could be evaluated along a range of possible axes using identical terms.

The analogue world of traditional liberal education, however, resists this ideal and is haunted by an irreducible aura, a residual authenticity, that even on some infinitesimal level precludes the perfect repeatability of a string of ones and zeroes. If your experience of a painting, poem, or sonata is identical with mine, then the object of that experience has been reduced to the information it contains and so can be replaced by that information or its quantifiable effects. There is no difference, in principle, between a resumé of that information as well as of its effects and the experience itself, and therefore the experience itself is expendable, replaceable. This is what fungibility means: there is no consequential difference between my experience of a performance of Oedipus and its summary. Thus, the argument that the humanities and the arts open us to experiences that are meaningful in themselves collapses before the insistent rationality of the calculable. If your experience of a painting, poem, or sonata is identical with mine, then the object of that experience has been reduced to asset of calculable information. You don't need to read Plato or Confucius: an exposition of the basic argument is the same thing.

Moreover, a flattening of the world to a strict economy of the quantifiable renders life both frighteningly meaningless and subject to the most extreme irrationalities, since what is not reducible to the logic of the commodity is excluded from the rational and becomes the province of faith, belief, and at its most extreme fanaticism. It is no accident that the neoliberal world order has seen a variety of religious fundamentalisms on the rise. The world becomes split between a ruthless economic logic and an equally ruthless assertion of pure belief with no room for discussion, no room for reasoned dialogue. If we are to recover the possibility of meaningful future, we must recover the possibility of a logos, a word, a logic, that embraces the particular in the moment of its universalization, that recognizes in the unrepeatable the possibility of freedom.

The connection between the digital and the neoliberal economy of the commodity, I would argue, is not accidental. Digital reproducibility is the predicate for a globalized capitalist culture: the dream of a universal market in which films, food, and fashion flow effortlessly across a digital pipeline. Adorno and Horkheimer's nightmare of the culture industry (1973) may finally find its realization in the fusion of Disney, Amazon, and Whole Foods with the Spelling report's vision of higher education as a "mature industry" (2006). Such a world—to paraphrase Benjamin (1969), the work of life in the age of digital reproduction! —is also necessarily that of perfect commodification, one in which use value has been all but completely reduced to the liquidity of exchange value, in which ones and zeroes have become synonymous with the flow of global capital.

This paper will begin, then, with a reading of Marx's definition of the commodity and of money as the universal equivalent. It will argue that the world of commodification and digitality must be resisted on multiple fronts, but above all by insisting on the universal particular, that is to say, on both the irreducibility of our experience and the simultaneous need to translate that experience into terms capable of being recognized by others and able to organize others for meaningful action. After this theoretical preliminary, we will then look at three examples of resistance to reductive fungibility: the absurd in Duras's Les petits chevaux de Tarquinia, Zen Koans as a spiritual practice, and the Socratic pursuit of aporia. These examples will lead us to a discussion of the need to resist the demand for commodification, which is implicit in the neoliberal model of higher education. The paper will close with a meditation on Aristotle's claim in the Poetics that poetry is more philosophical than history because poetry is both addressed to the universal and deals only in the particular. It is, I will argue, the realm of the universal particular par excellence and that what Duras, Zen, and Socrates have in common is precisely a radical poesis that offers an image of what a utopian resistance to our commodified fungibility might mean.

In many ways, Marx's understanding of the commodity remains, to paraphrase Jameson, the untranscendable horizon of the modern and postmodern world (1981: 17). The commodity is equally the most basic form of the digital universe. It is the world of experience reducible to its most basic quantitative (and hence iterative) expression: money, exchange value. The commodity in capitalist production and exchange—as well as in our digital instantiations, representations, and assessments of the capitalist life-world—functions as the fundamental definition of the object qua object, as what literally counts as real. The commodity is a logical necessity for the existence of the neoliberal life-world and its bedrock ontological reality.

In Marx's great logical fable, when the world was young, two producers stood before each other, each holding an object that possessed a potential utility for the other. I stand with my bushel of millet and you with your lump of iron. Initially, we are perplexed. Although each of us could make use of the object of the other, how do determine what would constitute a fair trade? How do we compare such incommensurable objects? According to what scale can we measure the possibility of their exchange? These objects in their sensuous qualities and their potential uses could not be more different. There is no practical situation in which the one could be substituted for the other. But through the magic of commodity exchange they become part of an endless chain of substitutions, in which each can become the equivalent of every other object in this universe, be it boots, books, or bourbon. What these objects have in common is not a material property shared by the things themselves. Their utilities are so radically different, their individual properties so fundamentally opposed, that it is only in reference to some third entity that they can become comparable. The one thing these two objects have in common, although in neither case is it a material property of the object itself, is the fact that they were produced, that they are the products of human labor. That labor value may have only a tangential relationship to the actual use value of the object for a given producer, but it has a direct relationship to the effort expended. Likewise, though we may think of certain objects as inherently valuable—diamonds, gold, and other precious objects—none of those have any exchange value until they are mined, refined or otherwise produced, until they enter the market place and assume their positions vis-ὰ-vis one another: a pound of flax, a pound of coal, an ounce of gold, a book, a poem, or a painting. As exchanges become more routine and less a series of one-off unrepeatable events, there arises a need to find a stable universal equivalent for the expression of the exchange values of a wide variety objects and hence to make all objects comparable and expressible in terms of this universal equivalent, which in turn becomes what we know as money.

In early forms, money is itself a thing of value, and we may fetishize its value as the reason money has worth: gold, silver, iron bars, or even cattle (pecus, "herd" in Latin gives us the word pecunia, "money"). But the fact that these various currencies are themselves exchangeable shows that they are but momentary instantiations of a more abstract and universal form which can be expressed in any symbolic mode of inscription: paper, plastic, even electrons. The universal equivalent can symbolize all values precisely because in its function as the universal equivalent it has no value in and of itself. It is pure relationality.

The universal equivalent or money form in turn makes possible large-scale production and exchange. I can hire a group of producers, pay them for their labor and realize in exchange a surplus value beyond what I have paid them. This makes possible not only my profit but also, and perhaps more importantly, the accumulation of capital, which can be used to build factories, digital platforms and other assemblages that magnify the power of individual labor. This surplus value in turn can be used to generate new forms of monetary accumulation through finance capital and other means of speculation that are ultimately disconnected from either the original use value of the object or the experience of labor that first brought it into the world. I can speculate on currency fluctuations, minor shifts in stock values, or engage in various forms of arbitrage that produce exchange value with little if any reference to an original act of labor that produced a useful object. The measure of a value that allowed one incommensurable object to be compared with another incommensurable object comes to replace the objects themselves, producing a flat plane of value in which widely disparate objects and activities are all rendered equivalent to one another and in which the measure comes to reproduce itself and have concrete effects in a world that it was initially intended to represent.

As Marx himself memorably expressed it:

> In order, therefore, that a commodity may in practice operate effectively as exchange-value, it must divest itself of its natural physical body and become transformed from merely imaginary into real gold.... Though a commodity may, alongside its real shape (iron, for instance), possess an ideal value-shape or an imagined gold-shape in the form of its price, it cannot simultaneously be both real iron and real gold. To establish its price, it is sufficient for it to be equated with gold in the imagination. But to enable it to render its owner the service of universal equivalent, it must be actually replaced by gold. (Marx 1977: 197)

Money becomes the measure of all things because money literally represents the digitalization of the life world. Things only exist in objective form within the digital/capitalist life-world—that is to say they are only abstracted from subjective experience and hence the world of opinion—to the extent that they can be expressed in quantitative and repeatable forms, which in turn renders only the commodity, or at least the commodifiable, the object qua object of experience. Hence, when we are asked to express the value added to a student's education of the reading of a given poem, the experience of another culture, or the development of creativity or critical thinking, this must be expressed in terms of a quantitative reduction, i. e., a "scientific", "evidence-based" approach, which can be translated into some form of universal equivalent allowing the comparison of incommensurable objects, which means ultimately it must be expressed in terms that are expressible in monetary form.

Within this life-world, the humanities per se can never have value. The point of education in the humanities is precisely to stand against the fungibility of our experiences, of their reduction to a universal equivalent, because the basic premise of that equivalent and the reason why it is so incredibly powerful lies precisely in the fact of its reduction. If we cannot measure the utility of reading a poem by John Donne, a novel by Toni Morrison, the Analects of Confucius, or a play by Berthold Brecht, then we cannot say the value added. That value literally does not exist. At the same time, to the extent we can express this value in terms of a universal equivalent, then the particularity of the experience of necessity becomes occluded. There is no material difference between the experience of reading the text and receiving the information communicated by the text, which logically means there is no difference between reading the text and receiving it in a predigested or summary form. Hence the text itself becomes superfluous as does the particularity of the culture from which it derives and in which it is experienced. Each is just another click on the Amazon or WeChat market place, another choice on Spotify, an option on a menu.

At the same time, the ability to be critical of the commodified life-world in and of itself becomes lost. There is no place outside its equivalencies from which to stand. An act of truly critical thinking becomes impossible because there is no locus from which the ironic perspective necessary to both accept the terms of communications and turn them aside from their accustomed track can be articulated. Yet this is precisely what the humanities does. It turns from the accustomed world in which our identities are pregiven and the object world is already defined, and turns back to the world per se, the world before the given object, a world in which the universal equivalent runs aground on the shoals of the Real. It does so from an ironic perspective precisely because it must speak in terms of the universal and the repeatable in order to be understood, in order for the cash value of its propositions to be received, and at the same time it must give those terms new values that cause us to question the fundamental nature of our given reality and to reveal an immediate terrifying and beautiful world underneath. Only in the face of this revelation can real change occur. Only then can we go beyond the already coded, the already given. In what remains, I want to give you three examples of what I am talking about before concluding with a reflection on how this joining of the universal with the particular lies at the heart of Aristotle's definition of poetry.

In 1953, Marguerite Duras published Les petits chevaux de Tarquinia, her last major novel before the groundbreaking publication of Moderato Cantabile in 1958, which announced her mature style. In this under-read novel from the period between her early Faulknerian work and the later elliptical style that was assimilated to what became known as the nouveau roman, Duras tells the story of five well-educated members of the French bourgeoisie on what appears to be a miserable and boring vacation in a small Italian town during a sweltering heat wave. In the midst of their complaints about the food, the heat, and each other, their flirtations and adultery, set in the period immediately following the Second World War, another very different reality intrudes and plays itself out in the hills above the seaside town. A young Italian whose job was to remove landmines from the surrounding landscape has accidentally blown himself up. His parents, peasants from the countryside, have gathered up his scattered bits and pieces and put them in a soap crate provided by a local grocer. Together they keep vigil on the crate, while the mother refuses to sign her son's death certificate without explaining why.

Each day the French tourists take a break from their bickering and ennui to pay a call on these peasants, bring them some food, and then return below. The juxtapositions can be very jarring. At one point, three of the women are discussing whether monogamy means you do not like to make love. Two agree and the third calls the other two whores, to which Sara replies, "It seems to me I could do it with fifty men." The scene then switches:

> The parents of the young minesweeper…were there still, waiting, in the shade of two sections of the wall. In front of them was a soap crate of average dimensions. …They gathered there all the debris they had found of their child's body. The crate was now nailed shut. There was a bottle of wine, some glasses, a loaf of bread, a piece of sausage, and some oranges. The old people were seated on the ground in front of the crate, the grocer a bit to the side. Two young customs agents kept watch while waiting for the parents to decide to sign the death certificate. They were also seated on the ground, in the black pile of stones from the explosion, in the shade of the other section of wall. …the shade of the walls was at this time so slender that they were seated with the others in front of the soap crate, like they were friends. (Duras 2011: 844)[①]

① All translations are my own unless otherwise specified.

In the seaside world below, words are exchanged like tokens. What is said often seems of little importance. The social niceties are observed. Boredom, anger, and lust are both acknowledged and passed over in a discourse that has very little purchase on the world. Social exchange is pursued with little acknowledgement of its real or imagined utility. But on the hillside, the terror of the Real obtrudes. Not in the world of discourse, but precisely in its lacunae, as we imagine the lumps of rotting flesh in the crate, whose odor is masked by the chemical smell of laundry detergent, and as the inexorable march of bureaucratic efficiency is stalled before the stolid silence of a grieving mother's refusal to participate.

In the moment of this encounter between divergent worlds, all the pretensions of normality that mask the empty exchanges of bourgeois life are brought up short before both the barreness of the Real and the bittersweet utopian promise of a world of simpler, more genuine human emotions. There is, on the one hand, the reality of a meaningless loss, the byproduct of a war now over but still producing death and destruction. The reasons the mines were planted are long gone, but the destruction continues, embodied in the death of the young minesweeper. That death, moreover, has been boxed and commodified like the soap once held in the container. On the other hand, there is the heart-wrenching loss of a child's death, the unvarnished reality of which is driven home by the peasant status of the minesweeper's parents, metonymically represented by the remains of their simple meal: some wine, some bread, a piece of sausage, a bit of fruit, a world foreign to the pointless bourgeois frolics on the beach below. There is also the powerlessness of the functionaries of the state before the parents' refusal to acknowledge either their authority or the finality of their son's death, to validate in the social Symbolic the loss torn open in the fabric of the Real. And yet, there remains a moment of possible community. A group of people have come together amidst the ruins, amidst their differences, come together in sympathy—a Greek word for "suffering together," for "suffering with." They "were seated with the others in front of the soap crate, like they were friends," as if they represented a genuine community of fellow feeling and mutual support.

It is this short circuiting of our everyday fetishistic reality that Duras's novel captures so well, the emptying out of the relentlessly homogenizing cast of conventional discourse. This is the primary function of the zen koan as well, a form of discourse whose impossibility is designed to explode our ordinary habits of mind or mindlessness, and indeed the false opposition between the two.

Koans take as their subjects tangible, down-to-earth objects such as a dog, a tree, a face, a finger to make us see, on the one hand, that each object has an absolute value and, on the other, to arrest the tendency of the intellect to anchor itself in abstract concepts. But the import of every koan is the same: that the world is one interdependent Whole and that each separate one of us is that Whole. (Kapleau 1989: 70)

The koan is the antithesis of the universal equivalent. Each koan is a little logical trap that at once invites analysis and pushes it away, always revealing more the limits of our conceptual structures than the possibility of there being a right answer to these maddening questions. When the student is asked, what is her original face, before her father and mother conceived her, she is plunged into both the confrontation with her own non-existence and a simultaneous urge to assert our continued identity. In the story of the monk Joshu being asked if a dog has the Buddha nature, when it is a basic tenet of Mahayana Buddhism that all sentient beings have Buddha nature, we learn that Joshu shouts "Mu" or "no/nothing." Does the dog not have it or is the nature that the dog has "nothing": a reality beyond any particular instantiation or coding? "Trying to solve Mu rationally, we are told by the masters, is like 'trying to smash one's fist through an iron wall'". (Kapleau 1989: 69 – 70a) The paradox and contradiction with accepted doctrine this little story embodies forces a confrontation with the emptiness that is both one understanding of the Buddha nature and its negation

In each of these little stories, we have both an acceptance of the necessity of the world of normal discourse, otherwise the case could not be posed, and the rejection of its fundamental terms. It is the power of the koan to both accept the world of things as given and to reveal the utter contingency of our thoughts about those things. It stands at the opposite extreme of commodified thought, of a theory of value that is based solely on the conventions that make operative the universal equivalent, in which my experience of the koan, or Duras's novel, or the world of things themselves is ultimately assigned a place in the world of being that is equivalent to a measure of iron, a pound of flax, or anything else that flows seamlessly through the world of social exchange. While Buddhist thought is as subject to mystification as any other form that becomes a codified set of conventions, including the wooden verities of conventional "scientific socialism", the moment of mindfulness produced by the simultaneous presence of absolute concentration and the radical questioning of the terms of the given world offers an important point of access to understanding how a world inexpressible in terms of the universal equivalent might appear (Sheng-Yen 2002: 49). In this regard it is important to keep in mind Shunryu Suzuki's definition of wisdom:

> By wisdom we do not mean some particular faculty or philosophy. It is the readiness of the mind that is wisdom. So wisdom could be various philosophies and teachings, and various kinds of research and studies. But we should not become attached to some particular wisdom, such as that which was taught by the Buddha. Wisdom is not something to learn. (1970: 115)

It is not a skill set, a group of competencies to be mastered. The radically disorienting questioning of the most basic ways we understand the objects of our life-world is a form of wisdom irreducible to the terms of exchange.

Where the postwar absurdism of Duras and the deliberate cultivation of no-thingness in the Buddhist tradition, on a certain level, appear to represent a rejection of rationality, that is less the case than a superficial understanding may make it appear. It is not so much that either of these discourses denies the cogency or effectiveness of a given logical system, of a given set of ratios and equivalences, as it is that they observe the radical contingency of those systems on a certain constitution of the phenomenal world, a certain givenness of the object world and hence of our place within it. And it is precisely the questioning of that givenness that Socrates, the founder of Western philosophy and its profound commitment to rationality, introduced on the streets of Athens. His request that each of us be able to offer an account (logos) of what we know and how we know it, in many of the most famous dialogues, leads not to a set of unquestionable verities but to aporia and perplexity. In the Apology, Socrates is shown to be the wisest of men only after he exhibits a superior awareness of the limits of his own thought and of his own profound ignorance by questioning the presumed experts of ancient Athens: the political leaders, the poets, and the craftsmen. His approach was deliberately disorienting and disturbing, comparing himself to a stinging fly striving to awaken a slumbering horse (Apology 30e), or being compared in the Meno to a sting ray:

> Socrates, I used to be told, before I began to meet you, that yours was just a case of being in doubt yourself and making others doubt also: and so now I find you are merely bewitching me with your spells and incantations, which have reduced me to utter perplexity. And if I am indeed to have my jest, I consider that both in your appearance and in other respects you are extremely like the flat torpedo sea-fish; for it benumbs anyone who approaches and touches

> it, and something of the sort is what I find you have done to me now. For in truth, I feel my soul and my tongue quite benumbed, and I am at a loss what answer to give you. And yet on countless occasions I have made abundant speeches on virtue to various people—and very good speeches they were, so I thought—but now I cannot say one word as to what it is. You are well advised, I consider, in not voyaging or taking a trip away from home; for if you went on like this as a stranger in any other city you would very likely be taken up for a wizard (Meno 79e–80b; Lamb 1967).

Far from providing answers to questions, Socrates often only gives us more questions and questions that we cannot answer, and yet in the end, those who stay around to hear, who do not react in anger, are driven to question themselves, to seek to know themselves, even to care for themselves (Apology 31b; Hadot 1995: 55–57, 105; Hunter 2004: 86–87). The Socratic logos—word, story, reason, account—as exemplified in the Platonic dialogues is not the ratio of accountancy. It is not a fixed set of equivalencies between already established entities whose values are known. Rather it starts consistently from the moment of a particular observation, then seeks to examine the possibility of universalizing that observation as a general rule or form of experience or knowledge (eidos) before returning to that understanding of universal form's inadequacy, and hence provisional nature, before the particularities of our experience. Though space does not allow it here, this pattern can be shown again and again throughout the dialogues, from the shorter aporetic dialogues to the more monumental "constructive" works of the Republic, Symposium, Theaetetus, or the Philebus.

And indeed it is precisely in this unceasing dialectic between the universal and the particular that the humanities, and poetry in the large Aristotelian sense, finds its purchase. For while I have been emphasizing the importance of the particular and the unrepeatable in contrast to the homogenizing and acid force of the universal equivalent, before which "all that is solid melts into air" (Marx and Engels 2012: 38), if you return briefly to Marx's logical fable, before the advent of at least some momentary general equivalency, you simply had two mutes standing before each other, one with his bushel of millet, the other with his lump of iron. The challenge is not to return to a world of dumb show and incomprehension, but not to let the relentless digital rationality of the commodity form become the sole or even primary index of our ontology, the thing by which we exclusively measure the reality of our observations, the meaning of our experiences. It is neither in the universal, which always must impoverish our particular experience, nor in the particular per se, which can never produce the repeatable and the intelligible but only the inarticulacy of the utterly unique and ungeneralizable, that freedom and meaning lie, as well as the possibility of human liberation, but only in their dialectic, only in the possibility of their momentary fusion and incessant disaggregation and deconstruction. It is this interaction which is the motor of history both in Hegel's Phenomenology of the Spirit and Marx's regrounding of it in the materiality of history, when as he says in the second postscript to Capital, he turned Hegel on his head.

Yet, in the cultural realm, the universal-particular reaches its fullest expression not in philosophy or science, but precisely in poetry, as Aristotle understood it, or, as we might say more broadly today, in literature. In the Poetics, Aristotle speaks of three modes of discourse, the philosophical, which deals with the universal, the historical, which deals with the particular, and the poetic whose defining characteristic is not a certain formal quality such as meter, rhythm, or even a given type of mise-en-scene, but precisely the ability to speak of the universal in terms of the particular, to tell stories or give voice people in accord with what seems probable or necessary. The poet according to Aristotle, I would argue, is less someone who finds himself halfway between the historian and philosopher, in a kind of mushy middle, than precisely the artist who is able to speak the truth of the universal through the evocation of the particular: rendering the irreducibly particular intelligible to a wide variety of experiences, and revealing the way in which universal always fall short of unrepeatable, concrete sensuality of that experience, even as it is what makes that experience intelligible, literally thinkable:

> It is clear from what has already been said that the work of the poet is not to say what has happened, but what sorts of things might happen and might be possible according to the likely and the necessary. (1451a 36 – 38)

That is to say, the poet's role is to speak of those things that could happen in so far as they participate in the larger, universalizing categories of what is probable and what is necessary, but only doing so in the particular.

For the historian and the poet differ not in this, whether they speak in meter or not (for it would be possible to put the matter of Herodotus into meter and, nonetheless, it would be history with or without meter), but in this: the one speaks of the things that happened, the other of the things that might be. Clearly poetry is both more philosophical and more serious than history: for poetry speaks more of things that are of the universal and history speaks of things according to the particular. Those things are of the universal, which are the sorts of things a certain type of person happens to say or do in accord with what is probable or necessary, at which poetry aims when supplying them names. History speaks according to the particular, saying what Alcibiades did or experienced. (1451a 38 – 1451b 11)

The poet is the writer or speaker who gives voice to the universal in the particular, to make them both speak in a singular moment. Hence, I would contend the role of the poet is ultimately to launch a reasoned and moving critique of both the universal and the particular, to display both their interdependence and the continuing need to deconstruct any fetishistic hierarchy of this opposition. It is on this ground that the humanities must stake their claim in the neoliberal university, a ground that refuses both false equivalencies and definitions of value that are predicated on and reproduce a commodified life-world.

In the end, then, we must not refuse rationality, but we must also accept that rationalities are multiple and that the choice of one interpretive grid over another has consequences and promotes or diminishes certain interests, certain investments. What the humanities does, with its focus both on the irreducibly particular as expressed through the universal and on the necessity of the universal to illuminate the particular, is constantly to put into question the necessity of any one of those grids, of any given ontology of the true. The neoliberal fusion of the digital with the verifiable and hence with the veritable is neither the only or the necessary arbiter of truth in any given instance, but is instead, in large part, an artifact of the hegemony of the commodity in global capitalism. So long as that is the sole standard by which value is determined and truth assigned, Aristotle's poets will not be able to defend themselves, and the lifeworld itself will be drained of all that is not expressible in terms of the universal equivalent. The resultant vacuum will offer not the emptiness of enlightenment but a space in which fanaticism and irrationalism can grow unhindered by the restrictions with which truth itself has been shackled.

Works Cited:

1. Adorno, Theodor and Max Horkheimer. *Dialectic of Enlightenment.* Trans. John Cumming. London: Allen Lane. 1973.
2. A Test of Leadership: Charting the Future of U. S. Higher Education, A Report of the Commission Appointed by Secretary of Education Margaret Spellings. 2006. http://

www. ed. gov/about/bdscomm/list/hiedfuture/reports/final-report. pdf.

3. Benjamin, Walter. "The Work of Art in the Age of Mechanical Reproduction." *Illuminations*. Ed. Hannah Arendt. Trans. Harry Zohn. New York: Schocken Books. 217 – 51. 1969.
4. Di Leo, Jeffrey R. *Corporate Humanities in Higher Education: Moving Beyond the Neoliberal Academy*. New York: Palgrave MacMillan. 2013.
5. Duras, Marguerite. *Oeuvres completes*. Tome 1. Ed. Gilles Philippe. Paris: Gallimard. 2011.
6. Hadot, Pierre. *Qu'est-ce que la philosophie antique*? Paris: Gallimard. 1995.
7. Hunter, Richard. *Plato's Symposium*. Oxford: Oxford University Press. 2004.
8. Jameson, Fredric. *The Political Unconscious: Narrative as a Socially Symbolic Act*. Ithaca: Cornell University Press. 1981.
9. Kapleau, Roshi Philip. *The Tree Pillars of Zen: Teaching, Practice, and Enlightenment*. Twenty-Fifth Anniversary Edition. New York: Anchor, Doubleday Books. 1989.
10. Lamb, W. R. M. *Meno. Plato in Twelves Volumes*. Vol. 2, Laches, Protagoras, Meno, Euthydemus. Cambridge, MA. 70 – 100. 1967.
11. Marx, Karl. *Capital*. Vol. 1. Trans. Ben Fowkes. New York: Vintage. 1977.
12. Marx, Karl, and Friedrich Engels. *The Communist Manifesto*. London: Verso. 2012.
13. Sheng-yen, Chan Master. *The Sword of Wisdom: Commentaries on the Song of Enlightenment*. 2nd edition. Berkeley: North Atlantic Books. 2002.
14. Suzuki, Shunryu. *Zen Mind, Beginner's Mind: Informal Talks on Zen Meditation and Practice*. Ed. Trudy Dixon. New York and Tokyo: Weatherhill. 1970.

World Literature and the Promise of Digital Publishing

Jeffrey R. Di Leo *

中文摘要 本文认为书籍批量出版的目的在于制造读者的需求，而按需印刷出版则把审美选择的权力还给了读者。如果这个时代的一些伟大作家能够抓住这个机会，自行按需出版作品，那么我们有更多的理由相信，出版界的未来将比过去更加进步和民主。数字出版为全世界的文学提供了这样的承诺：如果它值得被更广阔的读者群体发现，那么这样的时刻总会到来。

关键词 出版业；按需印刷；自行出版；世界文学；数字图书

Abstract This essay argues that corporate publishing aimed to manufacture the needs of its audiences, whereas print-on-demand publishing gives the power of aesthetic choice back to the reader. If some of the great writers from our generation were to embrace the opportunity to self-publish their work and make it

* 作者为美国休斯顿大学维多利亚分校英语和哲学专业教授，艺术和科学学院主任。担任美国多家期刊的编辑、主编，并担任美国批判交流协会（SCE）的执行主任。

available as print-on-demand, there is even more reason to believe that the publishing world of the future will be more progressive and democratic than the publishing world of the past. Digital publishing affords the literature of the world the promise that if it is worthy of a broader audience, it will have the time it needs to find it.

Keywords publishing industry; print-on-demand; self-publishing; world literature; digital books

The latter half of the twentieth-century was an active one in terms of mergers and acquisitions in the mass communications industry. Tracking the companies that acquire or merge film studios, television stations, radio stations, newspapers, periodicals, and book publishers during this period shows that each year an increasingly smaller number of corporations control more and more entities. In the process, the largest and most powerful global publishing corporations—companies like Random House and Hachette—each came to have more subsidiary presses than books published annually by the overwhelming majority of the tens of thousands of small presses in America.

The rise of neoliberalism in publishing in the latter half of the twentieth-century turned the writer's life from an aesthetic endeavor to a market-driven one. While small presses then as well as now largely remain immune to the lure of the market, this is not the case within the world of corporate publishing. The problem though is that many of the major small presses were swallowed up late century by larger ones during the ascent of neoliberal publishing.

In the 1960s, there were 183 mergers or acquisitions of book publishers including the acquisition of Random House by RCA, Holt, Rinehart and Winston by CBS, Popular Library by Perfect Film & Chemical, and R. R. Bowker by Xerox Corporation. In the 1970s, there were 177 including G. P. Putnam by MCA, Ballantine Books by RCA, Bantam by West Germany's Bertelsmann AG, and the merger of Scribner's and Atheneum, and Penguin and Viking. And in the 1980s, there were 213 with a notable increase from 1983 where there were 10 to 1984 when there were 29, 1985 where there were 30, and 1986 where they peaked for the 1980s at 40.

The increases in the 1980s complement the first-wave of neoliberalism ushered in by the economic policies of Ronald Reagan (Reaganomics) in the United States and Margaret Thatcher in Britain. Moreover, it should not be surprising that as neoliberal economic policy intensified in the 1990s with the second-wave neoliberalism of Bill Clinton (market globalism) in the United States and Tony Blair (Third Way) in Britain that the merger and acquisition frenzy during this period would intensify as well.

In the 1990s, there were a jaw-dropping 516 mergers and acquisitions, annually peaking with 71 in 1999—increasing again in 2000 with 80 and again in 2001 with 84. Highlights include Harper & Row acquired by News Corp. in 1990, Simon & Schuster by Paramount in 1994, and Ecco Press by Harper Collins and Da Capo Press by Perseus both in 1999.

Though there are many different reasons for these mergers and acquisitions of book publishers, including the need for mass communications companies to acquire more content, increasing globalization, and the rise of neoliberalism in the global marketplace, the effect on independent publishing was substantial. By 2010, Random House had 34 imprints in the United States alone including Alfred A. Knopf, Anchor, Ballantine, Bantam, Broadway, Clarkson Potter, Crown, Delacorte, Dell, Del Ray, Dial, Doubleday, Everyman's Library, Fawcett, Fodor's Travel, Golden Books, Harmony, Ivy, Kids @ Random, Main Street Books, Nan A. Talese, One World, Pantheon, Schocken, Shave Areheart Books, Spectra, Spiegel & Grau, Strivers Row Books, The Modern Library, Three Rivers Press, Villiard, Vintage, and Wellspring. Also,

Random House was now an imprint of Random House, Inc., or, in other words, an imprint of itself. By 2000, the estimated revenues from Random House, Inc. were 1.8 billion dollars, a figure that made them the fifth largest publishing company in North America behind only Scholastic (1.9 billion), McGraw-Hill (2.3 billion), Reed Elsevier (2.7 billion), and Pearson (4.9 billion).

One of the things that would change over the course of these mergers and acquisitions is that corporate publishing would have a much lower tolerance for publishing work that had a potentially small audience and limited market. Neoliberal publishing would come to favor authors like John Grisham whose work appealed to a global market of readers and shun the second work of authors whose first book had slim to respectable sales. Sonny Mehta, Chairman and Editor-in-Chief of the Knopf Doubleday Publishing group and Cambridge University educated, said "John Grisham is one of the greatest storytellers of all time." While this claim is debatable, what is not are the 250 million books translated into twenty-nine languages he has sold worldwide as of 2010.

Moreover, a consequence of these mergers and acquisitions was that it also became more difficult for first time novelists to have their work picked up by corporate publishers. The story here is only sadder for poetry and translation, which generally have a much smaller potential audience than fiction. Therefore, independent presses during this period took on a larger role as the publishers of new fiction, poetry, and translation, especially works that were innovative.

Good books for the neoliberal publishing industry are those that sell well and bad books are those that do not. Innovative fiction and translation might be good for literature, but it is hard on sales. Such is the world of corporate publishing, one that has enjoyed a steady rise since the last decade of the twentieth-century.

It should be noted while support for innovative fiction by the neoliberal publishing industry may be a grim one, it is pure sunlight compared to the plight of translation. This is bad news for world literature as translation is one of its primary vehicles. While it is often stated that only 3% of books published in the U. S. are translations, this number is probably inflated. Consider the numbers: in 2013, there were 542 translations published in the United States with 449 of them being works of fiction. This may seem a large number until one considers that over 50, 000 works of fiction were published in the U. S. in 2013. This puts the number of translations published in the U. S. at about 1% just among works of fiction, which is of course a much smaller number than the total number of books published in the U. S. in 2013—a number that was estimated to be over 1. 4 million.

Moreover, support of translation by corporate publishing as opposed to independent and small presses is embarrassingly low. In 2013, Penguin published 13 translations, Knopf published 5, and Random House only 2. By comparison, Dalkey Archive Press published 41. Another 28 were published by AmazonCrossing, a subsidiary of the book-distributing giant, Amazon, which is slowly entering the publishing market. These numbers reveal both the relative lack of interest by corporate publishing in translation and the relatively large interest in translation by independent presses. Roughly speaking, 1 out 5 translations was done by a corporate publisher, whereas 4 out of 5 were done by an independent or small press.

Amazon's entry into the relatively small world of translation publishing is somewhat the fly in ointment here. In 2015, it was reported that they published 75 translations—three times more than the 25 published by Dalkey Archive, the publisher with the second greatest number of translations published last year. In October of 2015, Amazon invested 10 million dollars into Amazon Crossing, which since 2010 has published 200 translations of authors from 29 countries writing in 19 languages. The translations are offered in print and digital, and in some cases even audio format. According to Amazon, the investment is a "commitment over the next five years to increase the number and diversity of books in translation."

Neither a corporate publishing giant nor a traditional small press, Amazon's entry marks a new chapter in the neoliberal publishing scene. While its motivations may be written off as merely a publicity stunt or marketing ploy, Amazon has leveraged its massive capital and market share to dominate a small but important wing of the publishing industry, and a large and vital area of the world literature scene.

The entry of Amazon, already a distributing giant, into the publishing world is ironic given that another thing that would change over the course of the mergers and acquisitions of presses had to do with the way warehoused books could be stored without significant tax consequences. Prior to the late 1970s, books returned to the publisher could be stored in warehouses and depreciated for tax credit. However, after the IRS's Thor Power-Tool decision in the late 1970s rescinded tax credit for warehoused books, it became less profitable for corporate publishers to warehouse books that did not sell. This meant titles often went out of print, especially titles of unconventional books.

In the mid-1990s, for example, out-of-print American titles included the following innovative classics: Robert Coover's *Origin of the Brunists* (1966), *The Public Burning* (1977), and *Pinocchio in Venice* (1991); John Barth's *Sabbatical* (1982) and *The Last Voyage of Somebody the Sailor* (1991); Stanley Elkin's *Boswell: A Modern Comedy* (1964); William Gass's *Omensetter's Luck* (1966); John Hawkes's *The Passion Artist* (1979) and *Adventures in the Alaskan Skin Trade* (1985); and Joseph McElroy's *A Smuggler's Bible* (1966), *Plus* (1977), and *Lookout Carriage* (1974).

The Thor decision had the unintended consequence of being a benefit to independent presses with a "non-profit" tax designation as they would become the refuge of much serious literature that was put was put out of print because of financial considerations. A great example of this was William Gass's *The Tunnel*, which took him over 25 years to write and was first published by Alfred A. Knopf in February of 1995. Unbelievably, Gass's masterpiece was soon after its publication put out of print by Alfred A. Knopf, an imprint of corporate giant Random House (though maybe this is no surprise considering that its president, Mehta, considered Grisham, not Gass, to be one of the world's greatest storytellers). In April of 1999, however, it reappeared in print with the independent, non-profit, Dalkey Archive Press, who had also reprinted another of Gass's classics, *Willie masters' Lonesome Wife* (1968) in December of 1989.

Such would be the fate of many other works of unconventional literature since the 1990s. Dalkey Archive Press alone reprinted around 90 titles in the 1990s including works by John Barth (*Letters* [1994], *Sabbatical* [1996]), Robert Coover (*Night at the Movies* [1992]), Rikki Ducornet (*Fountains of Neptune* [1992]), John Hawkes (*Whistlejacket* [1997]), Aldous Huxley (*Point Counter Point* [1996], *Antic Hay* [1997], *Those Barren Leaves* [1998], *Time Must Have a Stop* [1998]), Ben Marcus (*Age of Wire and String* [1998]), David Markson (*Springer's Progress* [1990]), Harry Mathews (*The Conversions* [1997], *The Journalist* [1997], *Cigarettes* [1998], *Tlooth* [1998]), James McElroy (*Women and Men* [1993]), Ishmael Reed (*The Free-Lance Pallbearers* [1999], *The Terrible Threes* [1999], *The Terrible Twos* [1999]), Gilbert Sorentino (*Imaginative Qualities* [1991], *Steelwork* [1992], *Aberration of Starlight* [1993], *Mulligan Stew* [1996], *Pack of Lies* [1997], *Sky Changes* [1998], *Crystal Vision* [1999]), and Gertrude Stein (*Novel of Thank You* [1995], *Making of Americans* [1995]). What is even more amazing is that reprints constituted over 50% of what Dalkey Archive published in the 1990s. Of the 172 titles published from 1990 to 1999, 53% were reprints (of novels, translations, and collections), 25% were first editions, 17% were first translations, and 5% were scholarly works. Since 2000, of the 558 titles published through 2015, 20% were reprints (of novels, translations, and collections), 80% were first editions, 54% were first translations, and 8% were scholarly works.

Entering the neoliberal global publishing industry in the late twentieth-century became less about the dreams of writers than the drone of accountants. It is an industry that has continuously been refined ever since the day Random House was sold to RCA. Now that Random House and Penguin have merged—and one in four books sold worldwide is the product of their joint operation—few companies worldwide have a higher global market-share for their product.

Corporate publishing is big business and growing every year. To enter into it as a new author or aspiring writer is both an honor and a horror. The honor comes with knowing that your writing is part of a lineage that goes back to the great writers of your press. Publishing with Random House, for example, places you in the prestigious company of Sinclair Lewis, William Faulkner, Gertrude Stein, Truman Capote, John O'Hara and James Joyce.

The honor of being part of an illustrious lineage though quickly gives way to horror if the sales of your first book are poor. Don't expect the corporate publisher to wait around five to ten years to see how your book fares over an extended period of time, let alone give you a second chance to publish another with them. Not only are books that don't sell well taken out of print quickly by the big boys, the new emphasis on "pre-sales" as determining the success or failure of your book makes the task even more daunting for the first time author.

The corporate publishing machine is geared toward low risk and high sales. The handmaiden to corporate publishing is not the perfumed hand of aesthetics or the golden arm of literature, rather it is the calculating brain of the marketing and accounting departments. Big Data drawn not only from sales figures and market analysis, but now also individual digital reading habits and social media activity are the key predictors of whether your book will succeed—and when it will fail. The publishing industry today is about providing immediate and maximal gratification to its consumers not testing the limits of literary taste or expanding the horizons of world literature.

The story of the corporate publishing machine is not a new one. Most writers today know the conditions for entry into the market and are aware at how these conditions have intensified as corporate publishing has grown in size and power. Publishing for Penguin Random House is first and foremost about selling books and making a profit for the global publishing corporation, not about the longevity of literature. Who has time to evaluate an author or book's contributions to culture or impact on broader social discussion? Rather, the global publishing machine privileges the immediacy of fiction—a world judged solely by balance sheets and units moved.

The safehouse for literature is not the global publishing machine, especially not the literature that was produced since the last quarter of the twentieth-century. Take for example one of greatest writers of the twentieth-century, William Gaddis. His first novel, *The Recognitions* was published by Harcourt, Brace in 1955, and his second, *J R*, was published in 1975 by Alfred A. Knopf. In 1993, Penguin (now Penguin Random House), reprinted both. However, since 2012, both Gaddis books are now in the hands of Dalkey Archive Press, a small press which will never put them (or any of its catalogue) out-of-print—a luxury afforded to it by its non-profit tax status.

But how many Gaddises and Gasses will be saved from the "out-of-print" death of the machine? Or, for that matter, how many translations can be done by presses that operate with very limited budgets? And where is the rage against the machine when it comes to its role in the death of literature and the avoidance of translation?

The global corporate publishing machine has the same role McDonald's has in our culture. Everyone complains about its ubiquitous global presence, the way it has put many mom-and-pop restaurants out of business and diminished our palate—but still billions of burgers are served. And the one in four books served by the Penguin company has far greater market penetration than the billions of burgers served by the clown company.

But the global corporate publishing machine taking the likes of Gaddis and Gass off the menu and avoiding publication of translations is an especially bad omen for literature today. So where can we look now for a reprieve from the machinations of the global corporate publishing machine? Aside from the small presses that are immune to the lure of the market, oddly enough, it may be the very technologies that have opened up book production to the masses, namely, ebook and POD technologies.

If the previous millennium closed with the corporate publishing machine at the apex of its power and control of the global book market, then the new millennium is quickly being defined by the potential of wresting much of this power and control from the accountants—and giving it back to the authors. The unprecedented opportunity today for authors to self-publish their writing provides them with the ability to have absolute control over the products of and profits from their artistry.

The down-side of DIY publishing is both that too many bad authors are using it as a vehicle to bring to light works that should remain in the dark, and that too few great writers are using it—an act with the potential to weaken, if not to bring down, the corporate publishing machine. What if Thomas Pynchon, for example, decided to self-publish his novels rather than publish them with Penguin? What would be the effect of high-profile acts of independence from and defiance to corporate publishing? Would such actions spur other great contemporary writers like Don DeLillo to do the same?

While I am not sure that Pynchon's corporate publishing Independence

Day would be widely celebrated by other high-profile and high-profit authors, it is certain that actions like this would be noticed by young and aspiring writers. His assertion of independence from the corporate machine would be a clarion call to the next generation of writers that the future of publishing is with the self-publishing revolution—not the world of corporate publishing.

In the hands of worthy authors, self-publishing can be seen as an act of defiance against the neoliberal corporate world—a world centering upon branding and prestige, not writers and literature. Thomas Pynchon needs the prestige of publishing with Penguin to validate his literary worth about as much as Joyce would need Random House today. Now, the financial part of the equation is another matter.

To date, few in the self-publishing arena have been able to produce the kind of profits of publication enjoyed by the big authors at the big houses. Sure, there are writers that have done well self-publishing their work, but they do not command six-and seven-figure advances for their work. In the corporate publishing world, solid pre-sales predictions equate to solid advances against sales. In the world of self-publishing, pre-sales figures are about as valuable to authors as the play money from a children's game.

The publishing machine in the new millennium is very different than that of the old millennium. In the previous millennium, the machine of publishing was an industry created around maximally profiting from artistic production. As the industry has evolved, it has come to be dominated by fewer and fewer companies with increasing levels of power, control and capital. In the new millennium, however, the machine of publishing is quickly becoming a literal one.

Technologies are now available to the public where for a small price, individuals can produce and reproduce on-demand print volumes of the same quality as corporate publishing. Machines like the Espresso Book Machine—

a machine the size of photocopier that can literally produce a bound book from a digital file in a matter of minutes—open up the potential for manuscripts to sit indefinitely in digital purgatory awaiting an audience to find them and print them out.

"With the EBM no book need ever go out of print, and any book in any language can be available anywhere in the world," said company co-founder and CEO, Dane Neller, in a 2007 interview. "More books will be published efficiently, i. e., supply will be matched by demand." "Bookstores will be able to reconfigure their floor space to sell faster moving, higher margin inventory," continued Neller, "and rely on the Espresso for mid-and backlist books."

Similarly, digital books are a technology that also allows individuals to produce volumes that need never materialize as paper products or warehouse stock. Machines like the Kindle or the IPad open up the potential for ebooks to be downloaded and enjoyed by readers in greater numbers than were ever previously seen by a generation that carted around books in a knapsack.

Since 2007, the year in which the Kindle and the Espresso Book Machines were introduced, the publishing world has enjoyed the rise of a new form of mechanistic existence. In addition, most new and aspiring writers are savvier about opportunities for utilizing these machines for their writerly endeavors than they are with those of the corporate publishing machine. Still, the lure of publishing prestige weighs heavily upon authors. It is seen most exploitatively in the efforts of so-called "hybrid publishing," which draws on the prestige of publishing houses to charge authors a few extra dollars to self-publish their work.

Hybrid publishing trades on brand recognition to bamboozle authors into thinking that by paying to publish their work with say a Penguin self-publishing affiliate, they are publishing their book with Penguin. In other words, that they are a Penguin author. This is the metonymic fallacy of neoliberal publishing. Though this fallacy is not limited to the publishing world, using brands and branding to lure in desperate authors so that the neoliberal publishers can make a few more bucks is one of its lowest and most predatory instantiations.

In the new millennium, corporate publishing means something much different to new and aspiring writers than what it meant in the last quarter of the twentieth-century. The cold soul of capitalism has finally run the publishing industry into a place that looks more like a dead end than the road to the future. Gone are most of the bookstores and the print review venues that were in the pockets of the publishing industry. What remains is a digital expanse that offers anyone and everyone the opportunity to not only self-publish reviews, but also to easily and affordably self-publish books.

Within this brave new digital world of publishing is the opportunity to rage against the machine of corporate publishing by embracing technologies for book production and reproduction that are outside of their control. The question is whether writers will use this opportunity to produce and disseminate important, innovative, and aesthetically challenging literary work or whether it will be more of the same. Hybrid publishing is a step back to the future of corporate publishing; self-publishing though is a step into a future where writers are in full-control of their work and any benefits that they may produce.

When a Dalkey Archive Press author, Svetlana Alexievitch, won the Nobel Prize for Literature this past fall, sales of her books skyrocketed into the thousands overnight. Nevertheless, Dalkey Archive, publisher of the translation of her *Voices from Chernobyl* (2005), had only one copy in their inventory. Upon news of the award coupled with an avalanche of book orders, Dalkey Archive sent their sole copy of her book to their distributor, Ingram, to scan. In less than 36 hours, hardbound copies of the title were ready to ship to libraries, booksellers, and customers. POD technologies allowed Dalkey Archive to provide a seamless response to the spike in demand for Alexievitch's award-winning book.

The international audience eager to read the Nobel laureate's masterwork had their demands met and the small press, Dalkey Archive, saw no downside from inventorying only one copy of her book. "Print-on-demand," said Dalkey Archive publisher, John O'Brien, "allowed us to get the book out in a matter of days." I can't think of a better story to illustrate the limits of corporate publishing—and the potential of digital publishing for world literature today.

So why not entrust world literature to more publishers like Dalkey Archive? Publishers who will not prejudge literature that is not immediately the darling of the market but are committed to its long run? Publishers who can leverage the flexibility of print-on-demand technology against a commitment to publishing serious and challenging literature? For some, digital publishing marks the end of books. While this may be the case, it also marks a new beginning for literature—the kind of writing that will be with us long after the flash of new fiction subsides and this year's best-sellers become last year's model.

My hope is that our welcome to the new machines of publishing is one where the aesthetic, social, and political dreams of writers are provided with absolute freedom and autonomy from corporate censure and control. Welcoming new and aspiring writers to the machine is to welcome them to the opportunity to find an audience for their work. It is a safe-haven for translations that bring literature from across the world to our doorstep. Works and authors who do not immediately inspire our wallets like John Grisham or Tom Clancy, but rather wait in translation for a decade in the shadows like Svetlana Alexievitch to garner the prestige and sales not afforded them by the world of corporate publishing. That her caretaker was a small press that utilized digital technology to meet overnight global demand for her books is a lesson from the future of publishing, not its past.

Corporate publishing aimed to manufacture the needs of its audiences, whereas print-on-demand publishing gives the power of aesthetic choice back to the reader. If some of the great writers from our generation were to embrace the opportunity to self-publish their work and make it available as print-on-demand, there is even more reason to believe that the publishing world of the future will be more progressive and democratic than that of the past. Digital publishing affords the literature of the world the promise that if it is worthy of a broader audience, it will have the time it needs to find it.

Works Cited:

1. Alexievitch, Svetlana. *Tchernobylskaia Molitva.* Moscow: Editions Ostojie, 1997.
2. Alexievitch, *Svetlana. Voices from Chernobyl.* Trans. Keith Gessen. Normal, IL: Dalkey Archive, 2005.
3. Bosman, Julie. "Penguin and Random House Merge, Saying Change Will Come Slowly." *New York Times.* 1 July 2013. http://www.nytimes.com/2013/07/02/business/media/merger-of-penguin-and-random-house-is-completed.html?_r=0.
4. Bowker. "Print ISBN counts, USA pubdate 2002 - 2013." http://www.bowker.com/tools-resources/Bowker-Data.html.
5. Di Leo, Jeffrey R. *Corporate Humanities in Higher Education: Moving Beyond the Neoliberal Academy.* New York: Palgrave Macmillan, 2013.
6. Fielding, Elizabeth. "Demand Surge for Nobel Prize Winners Books Handled with Ease by Ingram." October 19, 2015. http://www.prweb.com/releases/2015/10/prweb13030183.htm#!
7. Flood, Alison. "How Amazon came to Dominate Fiction in Translation." *The Guardian.* 9 December 2015. https://www.theguardian.com/books/2015/dec/09/amazon-publishing-translated-fiction-amazoncrossing-sales.
8. Gaddis, William. *The Recognitions.* New York: Harcourt, Brace, 1955.
9. Gaddis, William. *J R.* New York: Alfred A. Knopf, 1975.
10. Gaddis, William. *The Recognitions.* Normal, IL: Dalkey Archive, 2012.
11. Gaddis, William. *J R.* Normal, IL: Dalkey Archive, 2012.
12. Gass, William. *The Tunnel.* New York: Alfred A. Knopf, 1995.
13. Gass, William. *The Tunnel.* Normal, IL: Dalkey Archive, 1999.
14. Gass, William. *Willie Masters' Lonesome Wife.* Evanston: Tri-Quarterly/Northwestern University Press, 1968.

15. Gass, William. *Willie Masters' Lonesome Wife.* Normal, IL: Dalkey Archive, 1989.

16. Greco, Albert N. *The Book Publishing Industry*, Second Edition. London: Lawrence Erlbaum Associates Publishers, 2005.

17. Grisham, John. "23 John Grisham Titles Launch Today as Random House E-Books in North America." March 16, 2010. jgrisham. com.

18. Harris, Charles B. "Introduction." Special issue on independent presses and contemporary American literature. *Critique*, 37.3 (1996): 163 – 170.

19. Neller, Dane. "Interview with Dane Neller of On Demand Book—The Book Espresso Machine." Posted by Tom Masters. 26 June 2007. http://futureperfectpublishing. com/2007/06/26/interview-with-dane-neller-of-on-demand-books-the-book-espresso-machine/

20. Stegner, Manfred B. and Ravi Roy. *Neoliberalism: A Very Short Introduction.* Oxford: Oxford University Press, 2000.

21. Thompson, John. *Merchants of Culture: The Publishing Business in the Twenty-First Century.* Cambridge: Polity Press, 2010.

22. Totosy de Zepetnek, and Joshua Jia. "Electronic Journals, Prestige, and the Economics of Academic Journal Publishing." CLC Web: *Comparative Literature and Culture*, 16.1 (2014). http://docs. lib. purdue. edu/clcweb/vol 16/iss1/12.

The Maze and the Matrix: Fantasizing the Missing Other

Jacob Blevins*

中文摘要 本文考察了焦虑在拉康式“他者”中的整体地位。通过回顾最近出现在文化理论家、哲学家斯拉沃热·齐泽克著作中拉康式精神分析的弗洛伊德基础与拉康思想的发展，本项研究表明了焦虑是如何在幻想结构中发挥作用的，特别是幻想如何隐藏“缺失”。对拉康而言，缺失的缺失正是焦虑的典型特征。笔者使用了两部叙事性影视作品来说明幻想结构中的主观性和自我实现：HBO的《西部世界》系列剧集和电影《黑客帝国》（1999）。两部影视作品都表现了在被建构的现实中作为无法抗拒之存在的焦虑，焦虑在主体开始从这些现实中觉醒并遇到他者的力量和最终存在的时刻被释放，以及这样一种觉醒所带来对缺失的认识。

关键词 雅克·拉康；精神分析；斯拉沃热·齐泽克；他者；幻想；焦虑

Abstract This article examines the integral position that anxiety

* 作者为美国萨姆休斯顿州立大学英语系教授。

holds in the Lacanian Other. Looking at both the Freudian foundation of Lacanian psychoanalysis and the development of Lacanian thought as it has recently appeared in the work of cultural theorist and philosopher, Slavoj Žižek, this study demonstrates how anxiety functions within the construction of fantasy, specifically how fantasy conceals lack, a fact that, for Lacan, is the defining characteristic of anxiety: the lack of lack. I use two cinematic narratives to illustrate subjectivity and self-actualization within the construction of fantasy: HBO's series *Westworld* and the 1999 film, *The Matrix*. Both narratives demonstrate the overwhelming presence of anxiety within constructed realities and the release of that anxiety as subjects begin to awaken from those realities and to encountering the power and ultimate presence of the Other, and the recognition of lack such awakening brings.

Keywords Jacques Lacan, Psychoanalysis, Slavoj Žižek, The Other, Fantasy, Anxiety

One of the most prevalent concepts in contemporary literary and cultural criticism is the notion of "the Other". The concept is explored in various critical contexts using various approaches. However, despite its common usage, like many contemporary critical idioms, "the Other" risks becoming vague and undefined jargon that lacks the critical precision necessary for a full understanding of the implications of the concept for literary and cultural analysis. Part of the problem with using "the Other" as a stable signifier for critical discourse lies in the differing denotations of the term itself. Said another way, there is no single critical understanding or usage of "the Other", and the failure to understand that leads to "the Other" being the vague, conflated concept that all too often manifests itself in the critical conversation about alterity or other related discussions. ①

Regardless of such a danger, "the Other" is indeed an important and necessary term in the production and understanding of contemporary critical discourse. Much of the critical confusion, simplification, or misunderstanding of the concept lies in the fact that it has manifested itself in various critical contexts in different ways. Although the Other is frequently connected to an external presence, psychoanalysis often treats the Other as a component of internal desire and self-projection. The theories of Jacques Lacan offer us a slightly different appreciation for the Other and how it is as much an internal psychical negotiation as it is an external presence. The Other in Lacan has become a cornerstone for Lacanian analysis, but there has not been a thorough discussion of the role anxiety plays in Lacan's positioning of the Other (and *other*) in self-image and structure, despite Lacan's dedicating an entire year of his Seminar to the topic of "Anxiety" (Seminar X). Following Freud, who writes "The problem of anxiety is a nodal point at which the most various and important questions converge, a riddle whose solution would be bound to throw a flood of light on our whole mental existence,"② Lacan asserts at the beginning of his Seminar that anxiety is the topic that sheds lights on all the others:

> Anxiety is very precisely the meeting point where everything from my previous disquisition is lying in wait for you. You're going to see how a certain number of terms, which until now may not have appeared adequately linked to one another, can now be connected

---

① See J. Hillis Miller's book *Others* (Princeton UP, 2001) and Steven Shankman's *Other Others* (SUNY, 2010).

② See Freud's *Introductory Lectures on Psycho-Analysis* (*1916 – 1917*). Standard Edition, 16: 393.

> up. You're going to see, I think, how in being knotted together more tightly on the ground of anxiety each one will fall into place even better. ①

Of course, how we understand the key terms of Other and objet petit a (*other*) is of paramount importance for us. If we are to take Lacan at his word, we must understand anxiety to understand the Other and the facets that make it up.

Before discussing anxiety and the Other, it is necessary to have a sense of the distinct conceptions of the big "Other" and the little "other" and how those interact with the larger Lacanian realm. Lacan differentiates between the "Other" and "other" (the *objet petit a*). Lacan's Other (the big O other) is characterized as an unattainable source of desire for wholeness, a kind of transcendental signifier for the manifestation of desire. The Other is situated both behind the limitations of representation (of language for example) and within the inarticulable realm of the Lacanian Real. Lacan's *objet petit a* is the other the subject mistakes for the Other; it manifests itself out of our own self projection, our own self-reflective gaze. The other for Lacan is fantasy, existing only as a placeholder for our lack of Other. Although the subject's engagement with the O/other is rooted in an internal process of subjectivity, the displacement of desire to external markers (through the *objet petit a*) within the fragmented Symbolic lays a foundation for identifying the other outside of the self.

Anxiety may not have received the attention that concepts such as the O/other, the gaze, desire, and so on do, but anxiety is elemental in Lacan and to reflect fully on the role anxiety plays in the world of the Lacanian O/other a return to Freud is necessary. Freud's early work on anxiety presents anxiety as primarily a libidinal, physiological response to

---

① Lacan, *Seminar of Jacques Lacan* (Book 10). New York: Norton (2014), 3.

unsatisfied sexual desire, but Freud himself later recognized the psychical scope of anxiety. ①In fact, Freud considered anxiety to be a crucial point of psychical analysis as a whole: Freud separates the functions or nature of anxiety into automatic and signal anxiety, the latter of which is connected to the disintegration of the self, the former a kind of front line anxiety that alarms the subject of the possibilities of that disintegration. ②Like Freud, Lacan also understood the significance of anxiety and its function in the construction and projection of the ego. Lacan saw the immensity of anxiety within his model of development. Freud called anxiety the "nodal point" that when examined could offer insight into the whole of "mental existence." When Lacan writes that one will understand more fully his other concepts by understanding anxiety, by suggesting that his discussion of anxiety puts many of his other concepts into a clearer light, it may be concluded that no complete understanding of the Lacanian O/other is possible without Seminar 10. Even before the 1962 seminar, Lacan frequently cited the significance of anxiety, particularly Freud's concept of signal anxiety:

> Anxiety is not a sort of energy that the subject has to apportion out in order to constitute objects.... Anxiety is always defined as appearing suddenly, or arising. To each of the objectal relations there corresponds a mode of identification of which anxiety is the signal. The identifications...preceed the ego-identification. But even when this latter will have been achieved, every new re-identification of the subject will cause anxiety to arise.... Anxiety is a connotation, a signal, as Freud

---

① See Freud, *Inhibitions, Symptoms, and Anxiety*. Vol. 20. (1929) The Standard Edition. *The Complete Psychical Works of Sigmund Freud*. New York: Norton, 1990.

② See Jean Laplanche and Jean-Bertrand Pontalis, *The Language of Psychoanalysis*. London: Hogarth Press, p. 198.

> always very clearly formulated it, a quality, a subjective colouration. ①

Still, the 1962 Seminar is the most thorough treatment of the concept, and indeed *Seminar* 10 gives us much on the Imaginary, castration, the Real, object relations, the identification of the ego, and our current topic, the O/other. There are a few key aspects in his seminar on anxiety that are of particular relevance. First of all, for Lacan, anxiety arises not because of lack, but because of a lack of lack. In other words, when lack is not recognized, when the subject is too secure in his/her self-positioning within the structural confines of the Symbolic, anxiety is the result. As Charles Shepherdson puts it, "For Lacan ...if anxiety arises it is rather because lack has not yet been instituted for the subject.... it [anxiety] is rather the first incarnation of a lack that opens the field in which language will find its place.... Lacan argues that anxiety is the index of an Other that is too close or too full; it indicates not a lack to be overcome, but a lack that has not been fully established, and requires elaboration in order to be secured."② Patients do not suffer anxiety because they cannot overcome the distance between themselves and an Other, but rather they do not even understand the gap (and the resulting lack) and distance that exist between themselves and that Other.

While our ability to engage the Other directly is lacking, there is a functional role the object plays for the subject seeking to fill the gap of an anticipated identity castration (the loss of the perceived self within the Imaginary). What Lacan proposes is that the subject ultimately fixates on

---

① *Freud's Papers and Techniques*, pp. 1953-1954. *The Seminar of Jacques Lacan: Book* 1. Jacques-Alain Miller (ed.), John Forrester (trans.), New York: Norton, 1988, pp. 68-69.

② Charles Shepherdson, Foreword. *Lacan's Seminar on Anxiety: An Introduction* by Roberto Harari (New York: The Other Press) 2001. xlviii. N. 21.

objects that are negotiable, that is they can be exchanged, emulated, battled, and perhaps even overcome:

> First of all, there is the plane of the first identification with the specular image, the original misrecognition of the subject in his totality. Next, there is the transitivist reference that is established in his relation to the imaginary other, his *semblable*. This means that his identity is always poorly disentangled from the other party's identity. Hence the introduction of mediation by means of a common object, an object of competition, whose status will be derived from the notion of belonging—it's yours or it's [sic] mine.
>
> There are two kinds of object in the field of belongings—those that can be shared and those that can't. I can still see those objects that can't be shared circulating in the domain of sharing, alongside the other objects. Whose status leans squarely on competition, an ambiguous function that is at once rivalry and agreement. A price can be set on these objects, they are objects of exchange. ①

When the subject fails to recognize the true lack, the true separation between itself and the Other,② objects, the *objet a*, function as placeholders that subvert or conceal the presence of lack (i. e., they create

---

① Lacan, *Anxiety*, p. 91.

② Lacan identifies this inexpressible, unattainable Other as "the essential object which is not an object any longer, but this something faced with which all words cease and all categories fail, the object of anxiety par excellence." The Ego in Freud's Theory and in the Technique of Psychoanalysis 1954 - 1955. *The Seminar of Jacques Lacan*: *Book II* (W. W. Norton & Company, 1991), p. 164. Lacan also discusses anxiety in *Seminar IV*: *Object-Relations*, 1956/57, *Seminar VIII*: *Transference*, 1960/61, and, later, *Seminar XXII*: '*R-I-S*'. 1975/76.

a lack of lack in the subject). ① Renata Salecl states it this way: "[T]he source of anxiety for the subject is not the lack, but rather the absence of the lack...the fact that where there is supposed to be lack, some object is present."② This object, this *other*, blankets the lack; it gives the subject the false—and frequently temporary—identification with the Other: "The subject is also always bothered by the fact that the Other is inconsistent, that the Other is split, non-whole, which means that ... one cannot say what the Other's desire is or how one appears in the desire of the Other. The only thing that can ensure meaning to the Other ...is a signifier."③ Desire is situated in that object as the unconscious means for denying both the lack and the reality of inaccessibility to the Other. We never can get to the Other; chains of structural signifiers ebb and flow, circle, skip over, or gravitate around that Other: "The barred subject, the only subject to which our experience has access, is constituted in the locus of the Other as marked by the signifier. Conversely, the Other's entire existence hangs upon a guarantee that is missing, hence the barred Other."④ The subject who accepts the signifiers as signifieds, who accepts the others for the Other, exists fantastically. Because anxiety is a condition resulting from a failure of recognition, fantasy becomes intricately connected to it:

> ...it appeared to me, in what was said during our Society's recent meeting outside Paris, that something had effectively fallen into place in your minds concerning the structure which is so essential and which is called *the fantasy*. You'll see that the structure of anxiety is not far

---

① "In so far as it is an *objeta* reduced, of its nature, to a punctiform, evanescent function, it leaves the subject in ignorance as to what there is beyond the appearance." Lacan, *Four Fundamental Concepts*, p. 77.

② Salecl, *On Anxiety* (London and New York: Routledge, 2004). p. 23

③ Salecl, p. 22.

④ Lacan, *Anxiety*, p. 114.

from it, for the reason that it's well and truly the same. [①]

How exactly is fantasy and anxiety the same? Lacan is not entirely consistent; although fantasy and anxiety are intricately connected, fantasy is not the affect; it is the source of the affect or the subjective reality that is constructed around anxiety. If anxiety is indeed the lack of lack, then the more stable the fantasy is, the more the lack is concealed from the self, the more distance there is between the self and the Other.

In 1980, a year before he died, Lacan made the now somewhat famous remark, "It is up to you to be Lacanians if you wish; I am Freudian." Lacan, fairly consistently, stressed throughout his life that his psychoanalytic program, for lack of a better term, was indeed a return to Freud. By the time of his death, Lacan's clinical and theoretical assertions had taken hold and developed a life of their own. Lacan's statement suggests as much. Even late in his life and career, despite his own shift away from his early structuralist models of the unconscious and curative therapy toward a more post-structuralist position, he felt the need to re-assert his commitment to and foundations in Freud. The statement, even more importantly, suggests that the appropriation of his ideas by the cult of Lacan that had been firmly established by 1980 had somehow deviated from his Freudian base in significant ways. Part of the problem in addressing the de-Freuding of Lacan is that Lacan at times seems to radically alter Freudian concepts, despite his claims that they are rooted in Freud. We have to exercise some degree of care. For instance, Lacan's entire symbolic-, language-based approach to the unconscious, though often infused with new and expanded terminology, is fundamentally an elaboration of Freud's notion of displacement, condensation, and other aspects of the dream work. Regarding his own rehearsal of Freud, Lacan writes, "The point

① Lacan, *Anxiety*, p. 3.

here is not to imitate him [Freud]. In order to rediscover the effect of Freud's speech, I won't resort to its terms but rather to the principles that govern it."① This is one of the most significant statements Lacan made about his relationship to Freud; Lacan is explicitly asserting that despite the revisions and expansions in lexicon, the principles of Freud lie at the core of Lacan. Lacan understood this about his own work, but whether or not Lacanians themselves embrace this idea is another matter. Shoshana Felman expresses it quite well when she states "Since what returns in the Lacanian 'return' is precisely what is unassimilable in Freud, the return to Freud is not unlike the return of the repressed."②

What of Freud is repressed and then returned in Lacan is continually repressed by many Lacanians today. Slajov Žižek has become one of the primary torchbearers for Lacanian theory. He consistently writes and talks about various Lacanian concepts and invokes Lacan in much of his work. However, Žižek's Lacan is frequently estranged from much of the core Freudian thought that makes Lacan Lacan. Although he may, for instance, take the drives that bond sex and death together as crucial elements of the subject's desire, the implications of those basic drives often drift off into his own more Marxist field. As a result, Žižek even when he claims to be echoing Lacan is more Žižek than Lacan. British cultural theorist Catherine Belsey reflects this same view fairly succinctly: "I should say at once that Žižek is brilliant: prolific, provocative, a thinker to be reckoned with in the world that needs such writers. I differ from him, however, in finding his work more original, more inventive, and less Lacanian than he claims."③ In many ways this makes Žižek even more

---

① Lacan, *Écrits*, trans. Bruce Fink (New York: Norton, 2006), p. 241.

② Felman, *Jacques Lacan and the Adventure of Insight* (Cambridge Mass: Harvard University Press, 1987), p. 54.

③ Belsey, *Culture and the Real* (London and New York: Routledge, 2005), p. 53.

critically relevant, but Žižek's program, for lack of a better term, often needs fleshing out. The similarities between Lacan and Žižek are far less insightful than is the identification and analysis of their differences.

Although Žižek's many discussions of objet petit a and fantasy conform largely to the principles of Lacan's own, Žižek's Big Other deviates significantly or at least, one might say, branches off from the Lacanian source. Žižek's fundamental belief, particularly in his early work, is that the Lacanian Other is linked specifically to the power of ideology. For Žižek, the ideological discourse within which the self navigates is the fantasy that binds the subject to the Symbolic; what lies beyond that ideology for Žižek is the big Other: "the 'big Other' appears as the hidden agency 'that pulls the strings' and runs the show behind the scenes: Divine Providence in Christian ideology, the 'craftiness of Hegelian Reason' [...], the 'invisible hand of the market' in mercantile economy, the 'objective logic of history' in Marxism-Leninism, the 'Jewish conspiracy' in Nazism, etc."① What Žižek suggests is that the Other is the underlying, guiding power ideal that supports a system of ideology, a belief system. The system itself is the fantasy that suggests that the Other is real and is somehow attainable if the system remains intact—and such ideological systems are self-perpetuating, the fantasy sustains the fantasy. The most significant implication of this is that with this construct in mind, the fantasy gives validity to the Other, to this hidden agency. The challenge in Žižek—when considering Lacan's discussions about the Other—is that Divine Providence, Hegelian Reason, the market, objective logic, and the Jewish conspiracy are neither hidden nor a transcendental signifier for their respective systems. They may be the principles that fuel the ideological

---

① Žižek, *Repetir Lenin. Trece tentativas sobre Lenin.* Madrid: Akal. 2004. Qtd in George I. García and Carlos Gmo. Aguilar Sánchez "Psychoanalysis and politics: the theory of ideology in Slavoj Žižek", *International Journal of Žižek Studies*, 2. 3 (2008).

discourse, but they do not transcend the ideology; they are simply one object of that ideology and false Other. The true big Other, rather, is what allows these ideological guiding principles to exist in the first place; the hidden agency is not these "ideas" themselves but the desire to believe any system is whole and complete, to seek out some other—any other—to prevent the realization that the ideological system is not *the* Other and cannot be. It is in the fantasy of these ideas where anxiety irrupts.

When Žižek discusses anxiety, the Freudian signal anxiety that informs so much of Lacan, seems quite absent. Without the Freudian basis, Žižek's anxiety and its connection to fantasy becomes somewhat fuzzy. Žižek has claimed that anxiety is "the only emotion that doesn't deceive." However, Lacan states clearly, "What is anxiety? We've ruled out the idea that it might be an emotion. To introduce it, I will say that it's an affect."① Freud did characterize anxiety as *like* an emotional response, but not fully, and Lacan is much more consistent in considering anxiety an affect, a condition of fantasy itself, a result of the subject's commitment to the fantasy rather than to the recognition of lack itself. Anxiety is the result of an investment in the fantasy, the system of objects that hides the gulf between self and Other; it is the gnawing presence of a lack in a system—in a self—that works to prevent the emergence of that lack.

Žižek's various discussions of the Wachowski's 1999 film *The Matrix* have dealt directly with the issues of fantasy and the Other, and somewhat more indirectly with anxiety. These discussions are consistent with Žižek's more comprehensive analysis of film in general. He has asserted that film as a medium functions as a constructed illusion that allows us to live out reality from a position of safety: "It's only in cinema that we get that crucial dimension that we are not ready to confront in our reality. If you are looking for what is in reality more real than reality itself, look into the cinematic fiction. He claims

---

① Lacan, *Anxiety*, p. 14.

that cinematic elements such as music "numb the overwhelming anxiety of life...but the price we pay is that some radically authentic moment of accepting the anxiety at the very foundation of human condition is lost there."① Noteworthy is his specific reference to anxiety and reality (and by extension, fantasy); however, this is a far cry from Lacan's Freudian based anxiety that exists only within the fantasy. Fantasy does not numb our anxiety; it is the cause of our anxiety. It is our inability or unwillingness to accept or acknowledge the lack in our own desire, the distance the Symbolic places between us and both the Other and our Imaginary projection of self. These quotes from Žižek reflect not just his views on cinema, but they are also consistent with the manner in which he analyzes specific cinematic texts, which is evident in the 1999 issue of *Philosophy Today* in which he explores *The Matrix*, a film that depicts humanity as existing from birth within a constructed computer program (the matrix) [figure 1], created by machines to harvest

Figure 1

human energy. Humans, in reality, are kept alive and harvested in pods, as their minds live out their lives in the world they think they know is real. As the subjects are slowly taken out of the matrix (false

① Žižek, *The Pervert's Guide to Cinema.*

consciousness), and also out of the physical pod, they experience a dark, unwelcome awakening but an awakening none the less [Figure 2].

Žižek makes the argument, in summary, that the matrix itself (what is perceived as the real world) constitutes reality and there should be some acceptance of that, that the "desert of the real" that is the alternative for

Figure 2

Neo and the others who have existed within the matrix is not reality. Fantasy becomes real. But understanding Lacan's and Freud's views of anxiety, anxiety can only exist within the fantasy. There is a scene in which Morpheus explains to Neo: "You're here because you know something. What you know you can't explain, but you feel it. You've felt it your entire life, that there's something wrong with the world." This is actually the beginning of Neo's journey away from the anxiety of fantasy. Anxiety is not what will result from Neo's leaving the matrix, but rather his condition within the matrix. Morpheus becomes the Freudian (and Lacanian) analyst, sitting across from the analysand, who will deconstruct the illusion that causes anxiety. As the illusion is stripped away, so is the anxiety of feeling something is wrong with the world—though of course there is a whole host of practical problems with "the real world." Anxiety is not the defense mechanism, fantasy is, and anxiety the residual psychical condition that results. Lacan's idea of anxiety as "the lack of lack" that is tightly bound up with fantasy is fundamentally Freudian. Žižek's is not, despite the fact he correlates and situates his own views of fantasy with those of Lacan (and at times even those of Freud).

There is of course nothing wrong per se with Žižek's position on fantasy and statements about anxiety, but it is not exactly Lacan's position, still most narratives that deal with variations of alternate reality touch on the same representations that Žižek finds in *The Matrix*. The popular sci-fi, dystopian book by Ernest Cline, *Ready Player One* (2011), explicitly depicts subjects, on a large scale, inserting themselves into the virtual landscape of games, another type of constructed fantasy. Similarly, several episodes of the series *Black Mirror* explore various virtual realities and the subject's conviction to the fantasy of the Other. ①Adapting the original 1973 film, *Westworld* written by Michael Crichton, Jonathon Nolan and Lisa Joy offer one of the most intricate narratives of this type. Within a single narrative, HBO's *Westworld* addresses both the issues of subjects voluntarily, intentionally inserting the self into the system of fantastical others *and* the subject who unknowingly exists within the fantasy and thus suffers the anxiety that irrupts. In the original film Crichton depicts an elaborate park in which visitors come and live out various fantasies. The park is populated by robots (entirely human in appearance and action), but who are devoid of human consciousness—completely programmed to attend to the desires of the host. In the currently running HBO series, Joy and Nolan adapt the original, telling a story of not just the guests who come to satisfy their desires, but the emerging consciousness of the hosts (the robots) themselves.

---

① See particularly "Playtest" (Season 3, Episode 2), in which the main character volunteers to test a gaming system, but loses the ability to discern the game from reality.

The Man in Black (William), an investor in the park, has over the course of his adult life fully inserted himself into the fantasies of the park. We learn that he has re-defined his self-image over and over again; he has taken on the role of hero and rapist, of rescuer and murderer. The hosts in the park have simply been objects that serve his fantasy, whatever that fantasy is. But living the fantasy over and over again, in different ways, still leaves him with a gap. Displacing his desires onto the fantastical structure of the park gets him no closer to the Other—the missing object of his desire. He becomes obsessed with a symbol that is found throughout the park: the symbol of the maze. [Figures 3 and 4]. He believes that at the center of the maze is the true discovery: the Other he seeks, the signified behind everything else he experiences.

Figure 3

"But I think there's a deeper meaning hiding under all that. Something the person who created it wanted to express. Something true." (1.05

“Contrapasso”). The symbol of the maze functions for the hosts of the park as religious imagery that suggests an unknown purpose to their lives. William travels the park asking continually, demanding to know “What is the maze?” “Where is the entrance to the maze,” “What is the

Figure 4

center of the Maze?” The fantasy of the park for the guest, particularly for William who has explored every fantasy the park has to offer, is insufficient. It leaves a guest like William as anxious as he was before he first engaged the constructed fantasies within. He looks for what the other, the host, desires, but ultimately finds out that the maze is not for him. As Dr. Ford, the creator of the park, tells him: “The maze is not meant for you.” (1.10 “The Bicameral Mind”)

The maze represents the structured world of the hosts, those subjects who relive their lives in contrived loops, governed by the principles of the park itself. As Teddy, one of the hosts puts it: “The maze itself is the sum of a man’s life. The choices he makes, the dreams he hangs onto.” (1.06

"The Adversary") For Delores, arguably the true protagonist in *Westworld*, the maze is the path she must complete to reach freedom, a consciousness that is not dictated by the structure of the park, not dependent on the desires of the other, the guests. In her narrative loops, Delores has not recognized the gap between her choices, her actions, and her dreams and the untethered freedom she ultimately desires. She has not understood that there is something missing; like most of the hosts in the park, she has existed in a state of anxiety, the result of a lived fantasy not understood or recognized. When she begins her journey to recognition, she becomes like Neo and begins to sense that there is something not right in the world, in her own existence—a lack not previously understood: "I don't know. But this world ... I think there may be something wrong with this world. Something hiding underneath. Either that or there's something wrong with me." (1.04 "Dissonance Theory") It is in this moment of recognition that the desires previously held are now seen as somehow illusory, but even here the Other is still present, some unnamed thing "hiding underneath." But Delores now realizes the gap between her own subjectivity and the Other. What was anxiety of the unknown is replaced by a new desire to fill the gap.

The narrative of *Westworld*—with its binary of host and guest, the human and inhuman—demonstrates an aspect of fantasy that is only suggested by Lacan and Žižek, or at least not fleshed out fully. There is the fantasy we know and the fantasy we do not. Within the Matrix, subjects exist with desires that are constructed within a fantasy they do not understand; for them, the desires for the objet a are real and seemingly complete. Within the constructed reality of the park, the Westworld hosts live in a similarly contrived consciousness. These fantasies are the same fantasies of ideology that Žižek writes of so often—the forces that direct our desires—but there is a fundamental difference between the fantasy that subjects voluntarily and intentionally construct for themselves and the invisible fantasy in which they exist cluelessly. The entire Westworld park was built for the fantasies of the guests, for the guests to undermine the ideological constraints of their own "real" world. No matter how engulfed the subject becomes in the fantasy, it is never forgotten that it is fantasy nonetheless: William: "You're right. This place is a fantasy. Nothing here is real." (2.02 "Reunion"). Although what leads the guests to the park is their own recognition (conscious or unconscious) that there is something wrong with their own world, they understand the fantasy that is their real world no more than the hosts understand their own. Dr. Ford comments on the artificial nature of the guests' real world outside the park:

> There is no threshold that makes us greater than the sum of our parts, no inflection point at which we become fully alive. We can't define consciousness because consciousness does not exist. Humans fancy that there's something special about the way we perceive the world, and yet we live in loops as tight and as closed as the hosts do, seldom questioning our choices, content, for the most part, to be told what to do next. No, my friend, you're not missing anything at all. (1.08 "Trace Decay")

The conception of self outside the park, Ford suggests, is as formulated as what the hosts experience within the park. The guests escape their own maze by entering the maze of the park, but to no ultimate satisfaction, as William's disillusionment suggest. At the same time, Delores discovers that there is indeed something wrong with her world, and, for her, the dissatisfaction of her own sends her ultimately to look for the world outside the park, the maze she does not know. There, she hopes, she can find the Other behind it all.

The matrix, the maze, ideology—the Other is always present and always beyond our grasp. As subjects, we fixate our desires on those objects we perceive as real, as our own subjects of desire. These many others both substantiate the reality of our fantasies and suggests the lack inherent within those fantasies. Without a lack we understand, we are anxious subjects until we recognize that our desires fail us, or rather the objects we desire fail. When our lack becomes evident we seek out fantasies that we believe that the ego has constructed, our way of undermining the ideological systems that drive us, but the fantasies we know are as illusory as the ones we do not. Subjects in the Lacanian Symbolic are exchangers of fantasy; they exchange the fantasies they know for those that are hidden. Žižek suggests that our fantasies can be more real that what's real, the place where our true selves can emerge, but those selves are just as distant from the Other. These fantasies we create and live out on "our own terms" have already been made possible by the system itself. We can never be rid of the system; we can only enter a new maze that leads away, not toward, the Other within.

Ironic Enchantment and Postcolonial Futures*

Nicole Simek**

中文摘要 如今，既定的现实经常以痛苦或迟钝的方式限制着后殖民经验和想象力。而被理解为创造了多重的、对立的意义，或者一个无限否定之过程的反讽，却能够解决这些限制。反讽并不会规避和克服它们，而是在这些限制中做文章，通过浸入那些不愉快或无法忍受之中，重新引导那些试图掩盖或背离它的努力。但既定的现实也可以成为拥抱和庆祝的源泉，而不仅是对想象力的限制或痛苦的枷锁。只把反讽与去神秘化和痛苦联结在一起是错误的，因为反讽也和快乐、惊奇与着迷纠缠不清。本文将关注一种共同存在于很多法属安的列斯文本中对着迷的渴望，在这里反讽不仅是控制，还是一种能培育惊奇与欲望的方式。为了说明这一点，本文涉及玛丽斯·孔戴《维克托瓦尔，吾母之母》和帕迪克·夏穆瓦佐《埃尔迈拉的七个梦：马提尼克传说》两部小说，它们关注了持续存在的种植园，并将安的列斯想象中的社交状况作为某种解释性的典范以及后殖民未来的模式。这些文本依赖于一种游戏的能力，

---

* This piece appeared in altered form as "Thirsty Ruins, Ironic Futures," in Nicole Simek, *Hunger and Irony in the French Caribbean: Literature, Theory, and Public Life*. New York: Palgrave Macmillan, 2016.

** 作者为美国惠特曼学院哲学与文学专业教授。

以及一种对历史兼具反讽和着迷的情感接触。最后，本文提出的问题是，什么样的反讽模式最能满足人们对一个公正的“后”殖民社会的渴望?
关键词 玛丽斯·孔戴；帕迪克·夏穆瓦佐；着迷；瓜德罗普；反讽；马提尼克；后殖民文学

Abstract Current, given realities frequently constrain postcolonial experience and imagination in painful or dulling ways. Irony—understood as the creation of multiple, antagonistic meanings, or as a procedure of infinite negation—addresses these constraints not by circumventing or overcoming them, but by working in and through them, dwelling in the unpleasant or unbearable and redirecting attempts to cover over or turn away from it. But the given can also serve as a resource to embrace and celebrate, not just as a limitation or painful shackle on the imagination, and it would be a mistake to align irony solely with demystification and pain, for irony is also entangled with pleasure, wonder, and enchantment. This article looks more closely at a thirst for enchantment that cohabits many French Antillean texts, and the ways in which irony not only checks, but also fosters wonder and desire. To do so, it considers two novels that address the persistence of the plantation and its modes of sociability in the Antillean imaginary as explanatory paradigm and model for a post-colonial future: Maryse Condé's Victoire, les saveurs et les mots (*Victoire, My Mother's Mother*) and Patrick Chamoiseau's Elmire des sept bonheurs: confidences d'un vieux travailleur de la distillerie Saint-Etienne (*Seven Dreams of Elmira: A Tale of Martinique*). These texts hinge on a capacity for play, on an affective engagement with history that takes both ironic and enchanted forms. What modes of irony, this article finally asks, might best attend to a hunger for a justly "post" - colonial society?

Keywords Maryse Condé, Patrick Chamoiseau, enchantment, Guadeloupe, irony, Martinique, postcolonial literature

Current, given realities frequently constrain postcolonial experience and imagination in painful or dulling ways. Irony—understood as the creation of multiple, antagonistic meanings, or as a procedure of infinite negation—addresses these constraints not by circumventing or overcoming them, but by working in and through them, dwelling in the unpleasant or unbearable and redirecting attempts to cover over or turn away from it. Irony provides one means of approaching what Martinican writer Patrick Chamoiseau describes as a "mnemonic eschar"①, the sloughed off tissues that both cover over and painfully call to memory the wounds of history, of present pasts. But the given can also serve as a resource to embrace and celebrate, not just as a limitation or painful shackle on the imagination, and it would be a mistake to align irony solely with demystification and pain, for irony is also entangled with pleasure, wonder, and enchantment. This article looks more closely at a thirst for enchantment that cohabits many French Antillean texts, and the ways in which irony not only checks, but also fosters wonder and desire.

To some extent, the texts examined here appear to turn away from ironic multiplicity and opacity and to embrace instead more mimetic forms of representation. In this they share with much postcolonial literature a commitment to realism, or rather, as Celia Britton has argued, to forms of realism that are "reworked and renewed," that cannot be adequately described through commonplace oppositions between experimental and

---

① Chamoiseau, *Un dimanche au cachot*, p. 269.

realist, or resistant and ideological fictions.[①] Evidencing a strong commitment to photographic and archival documentation, these texts indulge in play but also take truth claims seriously. Maryse Condé's *Victoire, les saveurs et les mots* (*Victoire, My Mother's Mother*)[②], gives imagination and invention a strong role to play in building visions of the past and future, yet redraws boundaries between the referential and the imagined. Jean-Luc de Laguarigue and Patrick Chamoiseau's collaborative work, in particular their photo-essay *Elmire des sept bonheurs: confidences d'un vieux travailleur de la distillerie Saint-Etienne* (*Seven Dreams of Elmira: A Tale of Martinique*),[③] similarly relies on the documentary function of photography to support claims about Antillean pasts and futures. Yet both deploy irony to shift the affects and evidentiary procedures important to the reception of documentation as authentication.

While arguably flirting with uncritical modes of nostalgia and celebratory rehabilitation, these works invite us not so much to distance ourselves from projections of desire, but to traverse the separation of subject and object underpinning efforts at cognitive distancing and documentary capture that the past inspires. Both *Victoire, les saveurs et les mots* and *Elmire des sept bonheurs* return to a neglected period in Antillean history, the "siècle oublié" or forgotten century between the abolition of slavery in 1848 and the advent of departmentalization in 1946,[④] emphasizing present memory's gaps and silences with respect to this past moment. Condé's text confronts a willful family silence about her

---

① Britton, *Language and Literary Form*, p. 11.

② References to *Victoire, les saveurs et les mots* and Richard Philcox's translation, *Victoire, My Mother's Mother*, will be given parenthetically.

③ References to *Elmire des sept bonheurs* and Mark Polizzotti's translation, *Seven Dreams of Elmira*, will be given parenthetically.

④ The phrase is Micheline Rice-Maximin's, quoted in Green, "Maryse Condé's *Victoire*", p. 301.

grandmother's life and origins, while Chamoiseau and Laguarigue explore the industrial ruins and living witnesses that stand as traces of another age, traces whose decay discloses the mutability of the given. In addressing the persistence of the plantation and its modes of sociability in the Antillean imaginary as explanatory paradigm and model for a post-colonial future, these texts hinge on a capacity for play, on an affective engagement with history that takes both ironic and enchanted forms. What modes of irony, this article finally asks, might best attend to a hunger for a justly "post" - colonial society?

Melancholic Cravings

Both *Victoire*, *les saveurs et les mots* and *Elmire des sept bonheurs* revolve around specters and ruins, around haunting, even sublime images of destruction and survival, decay and resistant trace. Condé's story begins with a photograph of the maternal grandmother she never knew, an arresting image that provokes uneasiness and a lifelong curiosity. By her "Australian whiteness" and her kerchief signaling her lower-class status, this grandmother seems "doubly foreign" to the young Maryse, steeped in her parents' bourgeois and black pride values. Maryse is astonished to learn that her grandmother was a servant, a cook—a "genuine chef," her mother Jeanne emphasizes, as if to rescue her from stigma (2) —whose white employers financed Jeanne's education. In Condé's adult life, Victoire becomes a spirit presence who inspires Condé's own passion for creative cooking, but who also hovers in the night "like a reproach," waiting for the nomadic writer to take an interest in her life and embark on "the only voyage that counts," the "internal voyage" into the self (16, 2). The mysterious complexity of this presence lingers, breaking through her own mother's rare, clichéd descriptions of the stalwart matriarch, the "matador woman" and *poto-mitan* of Antillean lore (4), and urging Condé to "follow her footsteps" (16; *emprunter sa trace*). *Elmire*, a collaborative photo-text combining a mystical tale about Saint-Étienne rum with portraits of residents in the surrounding area, also tells the story of a ghost. Written in a first-person voice said to be that of an elderly worker from the Saint-Étienne rum factory, the text relates the distillery workers' encounters with Elmira, a mysterious and almost divine apparition who reveals herself on rare and unforeseeable occasions to those who savor Saint-Étienne rum in just the right way. A dazzling Creole beauty, who appears slightly different to each person who sees her, Elmira leaves everyone who glimpses her unsuccessfully guzzling rum in a desperate attempt to experience this vision one more time, while she leaves readers suspecting that she is merely a projection of frustrated desire, a vision whose beauty hides impotence and frustration.

In both texts, these haunting figures emerge in a present moment portrayed in some ways as broken. *Elmire*'s monochromatic portraits of elderly residents, interwoven with the text, recall that time is slipping away, but the color photographs of Habitation Saint-Etienne's "silence ... age, rust" (67), and peeling paint, its cracking walls with their "crown of ferns" (52) and its rickety windows intensify a sense of wistfulness for an era of lost productivity. Condé's text, for its part, considers the divergent paths history might have taken and invites the reader to compare them. If she asks somewhat tongue-in-cheek what "would have been [her] relation to [herself], [her] vision of [her] island, of the Antilles, and of the world more generally," had she had a living grandmother who, like the stereotypical Creole ideal, had cherished her and told her "sweet myths of the past," Condé also wonders more somberly what an alternate history might have meant to Victoire herself, and to her daughter, Condé's mother, Jeanne:

> With her meager resources, [Victoire] managed to force open the doors of the burgeoning black bourgeoisie for her daughter. But was it really worth it in the end? That is the real question I ask myself. That ample faculty my mother had for suffering and torturing herself, which she left to all of us—Victoire was the cause. Thinking she was acting for the best, she condemned my mother to live her childhood in solitude and ostracism, which had a considerable influence not only on her character and her behavior, but also on that of her descendants. (4)

The photographic scenes that preoccupy Condé, Chamoiseau, and Laguarigue function as phantoms, historical fragments and material traces that seem to call out for theorization, that present an alluring hermeneutic puzzle. As a precarious, endangered trace, these ruinous scenes provoke a sense of urgency, the need to preserve or recover a history on the brink of total disappearance. Viewed as well as an obstinate, resilient presence, phantoms and ruins evoke defiance, perhaps defiance to theorization itself, a stumbling block to narrative. In either case, the ruin evokes a melancholic longing for repair—for Elmira, who will restore "ruined dreams" (30), for connections missed and paths not taken.

In setting out to retrace the paths of the past, these authors inscribe their works in strong Caribbean literary tradition, emphasizing the archeological work literature must do to unearth a memory unrepresented in written history or public monument. ① Both texts frame their work as one of following "traces," a rich term evoking paths worn into the landscape and, more generally, marks and residues both material and immaterial. For

---

① See Moudileno, "Archéologie du cachot," for an insightful discussion tracing this theme in the work of Chamoiseau, who is indebted to Glissant's thinking on landscape, archeology, and the lacuna of "official" history.

Chamoiseau and Laguarigue, the landscape must itself be tracked and caught by surprise, if its meanings are to be released from the storehouse of memory: "Take landscapes unawares. Understand them. Lead divination with an innocent gaze. Pace (above the tangible map of light and shadow) along traces and details that are like memoirs." (51; *Surprendre les paysages. Les comprendre. Mener divination d'un regard innocent. Arpenter (dessus la carte sensible des lumières et des ombres) ces traces et ces détails qui sont comme des mémoires*). Surveying the land means going beyond traditional maps, and is more akin to an occult art than a science, an act of divining that requires a particular kind of disposition and perspective.

The landscape takes the place of history, and within it, the old distillery, partially invaded by vegetation, features as both a part of nature and an oddity, distinct from it. Derek Walcott famously described the Caribbean's "absence of ruins" in an early poem, and in his 1992 Nobel Lecture he returned to the theme, noting, "The sigh of History rises over ruins, not over landscapes, and in the Antilles there are few ruins to sigh over, apart from the ruins of sugar estates and abandoned forts."① In his 1981 work *Caribbean Discourse*, Édouard Glissant took up this erasure of collective memory as a troubling analytical problem, the problem of making visible a "reality that is so often hidden from view."② Glissant points to the need to look to the landscape itself for traces of this suppressed past: "History," he writes, "is spread out beneath this surface, from the mountains to the sea, from the forest to the beaches.... (Our landscape is its own monument: its meaning can only be traced on the underside. It is all history)."③ Here, the absence of the ruin does not obviate the task of

① Derek Walcott, "Nobel Lecture". See also Walcott, "The Royal Palms".

② Glissant, *Caribbean Discourse*, p. 2.

③ Ibid., p. 11.

excavation, but shifts the location of the surface to be probed and highlights its urgency all the more. For Glissant, "the Caribbean writer must 'dig deep' into this [collective] memory, following the latent signs that he has picked up in the everyday world."①

Walcott's Nobel lecture points, however, to a different sort of analytical problem, which is not so much the difficulty in piecing together a history that has been suppressed in Western accounts and also physically erased, swallowed up by tropical vegetation, but rather the problem of theorizing from the ruin, from the assumption that the present constitutes a ruin, a fragmented trace of a lost whole. Walcott's speech relates an afternoon spent in the village of Felicity, Trinidad, watching the villagers prepare for the Hindu performance of Ramleela, a festival during which the life of Lord Ram is reenacted to show the purpose of his incarnation and to celebrate the triumph of good over evil. Describing the preparations, he remarks on a particular sign he takes as a ruin:

> Under an open shed on the edge of the field, there were two huge armatures of bamboo that looked like immense cages. They were parts of the body of a god, his calves or thighs, which, fitted and reared, would make a gigantic effigy. This effigy would be burnt as a conclusion to the epic. The cane structures flashed a predictable parallel: Shelley's sonnet on the fallen statue of Ozymandias and his empire, that "colossal wreck" in its empty desert. ②

This "predictable parallel" produces ironic results. Perceiving the effigy as a ruin provokes a Romantic response—a response of melancholic meditation and critical distance from the performers taking up their costumes

---

① Glissant, *Caribbean Discourse*, p. 64.

② Derek Walcott, "Nobel Lecture".

and roles in the cane fields before him. Yet this perception comes to annul itself. Ruminating over his lack of familiarity with the epic about to be performed, Walcott comes to describe his own experience as an experience of misperception:

> It was as if, on the edge of the Central Plain, there was another plateau, a raft on which the *Ramayana* would be poorly performed in this ocean of cane, but that was my writer's view of things, and it is wrong. I was seeing the *Ramleela* at Felicity as theatre when it was faith.... They believed in what they were playing, in the sacredness of the text, the validity of India, while I, out of the writer's habit, searched for some sense of elegy, of loss, even of degenerative mimicry in the happy faces of the boy-warriors or the heraldic profiles of the village princes.... I was filtering the afternoon with evocations of a lost India, but why "evocations"? Why not "celebrations of a real presence"? Why should India be "lost" when none of these villagers ever really knew it, and why not "continuing," why not the perpetuation of joy ...? Why was I not letting my pleasure open its windows wide?①

Walcott frames the problem as a tension between affective dispositions, a tension between the melancholic "sigh of History" and the pleasure whose windows that sigh shuts, a pleasure described later as the ecstasy of poiesis itself. To perceive a ruin is to see with the eyes of History, with a capital H, a History that, as Walcott puts it, "can alter the eye and the moving hand to confirm a view of itself."② In other words, it is to mistake an absence for a lack, to project a loss from a particular vantage point that

① Derek Walcott, "Nobel Lecture".

② Ibid.

conceives of plenitude in specific ways. Walcott's denial of his own "writer's habit" seems to go so far as to deny or reject mediation; Walcott posits that the correct reading of the scene is to read it as faith, not mediated performance—and pleasurable participation, rather than distanced melancholia, is the proper response to it. He asks himself why he, too, doesn't open his windows to pleasure.

At the same time, Walcott seeks to retain the notion of an originary fragmentation, likening the culture and creativity of the Caribbean to the glue with which one lovingly joins together the pieces of a broken vase "Antillean art is this restoration of our shattered histories, our shards of vocabulary, our archipelago becoming a synonym for pieces broken off from the original continent."① Perceiving the Antilles, and its art, becomes, then, a matter of both remembering—of mediating—and of forgetting this original moment of ruination, of attending to both pain and pleasure, or what Walcott describes as "the pain that is joy."② In this sense, the ruin invites not so much a hermeneutic quest to reconstitute its original shape as an attentiveness to the present process of joining, to the qualities of the present mosaic and the forces that bind it.

Faith and fiction

In giving such attention to these processes of joining, *Elmire des sept bonheurs* and *Victoire, les saveurs et les mots* mediate critical reflection and affect in inventive ways, playing in particular on the permeability of enchantment and disenchantment in their ironic engagement with the ruins of

① Derek Walcott, "Nobel Lecture".

② Ibid.

modernity. [①] *Elmire* displays its mosaic techniques explicitly in its format, calling attention to the joints between multiple portraits, material photographic traces of community sutured together by the whimsical tale and also bound, physically, into the single object that is the book. As Maeve McCusker notes, the hybridity observable on the formal level of the book extends, through the collaboration between Chamoiseau and Laguarigue, to "the very conception of the creative act ...Indeed, not only are text and image juxtaposed in these works, but Laguarigue's background, as a member of the white *béké* caste, inflects the collaboration with a sense of racial and social hybridity." [②] This collaborative relationship extends to the community as well, and is most visible in the photographs included in the book. Pages of text alternate, in the original French edition, with posed portraits of residents of the area, who are acknowledged as "commanders of memory" and thanked at the start of the volume. [③] The volume closes with a series of color shots of the run-down Saint-Étienne distillery and surrounding buildings, accompanied by short, fanciful and elegiac

---

① For the notion of ironic enchantment as a self-reflexive approach to modernity, I am indebted to Michael Saler's "Modernity, Disenchantment, and the Ironic Imagination." See also Landy and Saler, *The Re-enchantment of the World.*

② McCusker, *Patrick Chamoiseau*, p. 16.

③ The English edition format is significantly different. The size of the book has been scaled down, and all of the photographs grouped at the end of the volume, rather than interwoven with the text. The order of the portraits has also been changed, and captions identifying them have been removed in the English version (page references have instead been given in the opening acknowledgements). Chamoiseau's name, which appears as a signature on page 49 of the French, at the end of the worker's "confidences" but before the color shots and accompanying text, has also been removed in the English. The most consequential alteration is perhaps the one made to the front cover: the French version bears a black and white photograph of an older man in a button-down shirt with his hands at the side of his face in contemplation, while the English replaces this with a color painting of a woman holding a flower, set against a tropical backdrop, in a thin dress whose strap is falling down her shoulder (a painting that appears on the back cover of the French). In moving this image to the front cover, the English emphasizes place and erotic femininity, while the French emphasizes the contemplative gaze and the ambiguity of its object and location.

captions. This closing section serves as a seam, an addendum that marks both a separation and a continuation.

On an affective level, *Elmire*'s emphasis on whimsical enjoyment and unruly humor competes with what we might call a sobering or poignant documentary imperative—a demand for realist or stable representations of marginalized peoples and histories, a demand for an aesthetics that can be put to the service of particular political ends. This competition first seems to express itself as a tension between the photographs and the written text, whose contrasting tones have struck a number of reviewers. The text has been called "savory" (savoureux)① and "luscious,"② a "tongue-in-cheek" tale of "nirvana,"③ while the photographs are commonly described as "striking" (Kirkus), "soulful, somber portraits" (Steinberg) marked by a "poignant humbleness" (une poignante humanité).④ That readers have perceived this to be a tension or a puzzle is both significant but also not conclusive, for we cannot discount the way in which strangeness can be coopted and read as "savory" in itself. As Celia Britton argues, the publishing industry that markets postcolonial work as desirable for its exotic otherness can usefully be viewed as an ideological apparatus, but one, importantly, whose ideological force "lies not in selling illusions—that is, illusory, because exotic, representations—but in interpellating its audience as consumers."⑤ If, she continues, "earlier institutions of imperialism interpellated the French ideological subject as guardian of the values of French civilization … in the globalized postcolonial world s/he is interpellated as first and foremost a consumer: more specifically, the

① Kwateh, "Elmire au bonheur des hommes".

② Steinberg, "Forecasts: Fiction," p. 65.

③ Kirkus Reviews, "Seven Dreams of Elmira".

④ Catinchi, "Livraisons".

⑤ Britton, *Language and Literary Form*, p. 60.

consumer of a commodified exotic culture."① In other words, commodification does not merely rely on the content of a representation, but functions by appealing to particular modes of subjectivity and action, modes that may be at odds with the messages we may read into the content. A text's performance of irony succeeds to varying degrees to the extent that it hails readers differently, that it calls them into different modes of relation, cognitively and affectively. In the case of *Elmire*, if the tale appeals to exotic appetites,② the portraits seem to function, for French and American reviewers, at least, as a sort of check on guilty pleasures, drawing the reader back into somber matters and warning against the dangers of succumbing to Elmira's charms. ③ If the written tale is marked by whimsy, the somber photographic testimony creates a sort of ironic puzzle, clashing with the lighthearted tone and inviting archeological excavation of the type Glissant speaks in *Caribbean Discourse*.

Reading irony into the text also hinges largely on the ways in which Elmira herself is figured in it. The narrator first introduces her in the text as "the one absence that we all share" (15), alerting us both to her enigmatic presence and the extent to which that presence may be an illusion. As we learn of the ways in which she embodies projected desires, she begins to look more and more like a lure, a trap, perhaps a fetishized commodity—like the Creole beauty portrayed on the Saint-Étienne label itself—that Chamoiseau ironizes and invites us to critique. Does the book really

---

① Britton, *Language and Literary Form*, p. 60.

② The French edition's status as a "beau livre," an illustrated, large-format display object or coffee-table book (the term translates literally to "beautiful book"), arguably reinforces its appeal as an object to be savored or consumed rather than engaged.

③ It is perhaps not insignificant that the French newspaper of record *Le Monde* chose some of these photos to illustrate the special 1998 dossier commemorating the 150th anniversary of the 1848 abolition of slavery in which the book review is published. This dossier includes historical documents (including, for example, an article by Victor Schoelcher) and contemporary commentaries; the photos, which bear no names, dates, or captions, seem to hover between past and present.

celebrate Elmira at all? Is the point of the text rather to move us beyond a helpless wait for alcohol-induced ecstasy? The portraits, however, would seem to trouble this nascent hermeneutics of suspicion by anchoring the narrative in the lives and beliefs of real people. In seemingly arresting ironic play by reasserting sober realities, the photographs function to encourage a hermeneutics of faith. Such an approach might read the text less as ironic lesson and rather as an attempt to document or testify to Antillean ways of life, particularly those ways of life in danger of disappearing from memory.

Photographer Jean-Luc de Laguarigue has endorsed such a reading of his art. A descendent of one of the economically powerful, *béké* (white minority planter) families, and one who has publically taken issue with his class's ongoing implication in economic inequality, Laguarigue characterizes his work as a "photographic quest" to "understand and render the complexity of Martinican society," and to create in its attention to memory traces what Édouard Glissant calls a "prophetic vision of the past."① He features interiors in much of his work, and we see people posing before the religious icons, clocks, television sets, and family photos with which they decorate their own homes. The choice of black and white for these portraits contributes to the sense that these images index a reality that is passing away, like the fabled rum and the bygone world that produced it. Documentation does not merely capture this fleeting world, for this photography constitutes an "alchemy," a "work of memory" that does not give us a "key" to unlocks the past, but that constitutes instead "a condition that is essential for the kind of expansion of consciousness that we need to attain" (*une condition essentielle à l'élargissement de la conscience auquel il nous faut parvenir*).② Yet photography also remains anchored in the real and demands faithfulness to it; new futures can be imagined, or

① Laguarigue, "Un autre monde." My translation.

② Ibid.

prophesied, but they must unfold from and take account of real, existing conditions.

Documentation takes on an explicit but ambiguous importance in Condé's narrative as well, and one that stands out by comparison to Condé's previous fictions. ① Opening with an autobiographical anecdote explaining how she became interested in gathering information about her grandmother (described in French as her resolve to "[se] documenter sur Victoire Quidal" [16]), the narrative then moves to late nineteenth-century Marie-Galante, weaving a story about Condé's family, and the social, cultural, and economic relations shaping their unfolding experiences, in which the line between invention and fact comes in and out of focus. As Laurie Corbin notes: "It is obvious that there is much that [Condé] cannot know, and the story is filled with details of a character's thoughts or a private conversation that are obviously not available, and thus imagined. At the same time she makes it clear that she has researched as much as possible her grandmother's life and those who knew her through interviews and some written documentation."② Condé's initial comment that after many years of travel, she now has "the time" (*le loisir*) to retrace Victoire's steps takes on a strong sense as the narrative unfolds, for what such a journey requires is a great deal of legwork as well as the leisure to sit with the sparse details that remain and attempt to inhabit a perspective and experience far removed from her own. Frequently, Condé signals this distance between present and past by naming the sources of various pieces of information or signaling their absence ("nous ignorons..." "mes recherches ne m'ont rien appris sur..."), commenting directly and indirectly on their

---

① Mary Jean Green observes that "historical references and attribution to sources are much more frequent in Victoire than had been the case in Condé's earlier, fictionalized family chronicles" (Green, "Maryse Condé's *Victoire*", p. 302).

② Corbin, "The Return To and Beyond the Mother", p. 235.

reliability and their perspective.

The first few paragraphs that delve into this past subtly frame the work of research as a dance between proximity and distance. The narration begins with a general geographic description— "In the hamlet of La Treille on the island of Marie-Galante, not far from Grand-Bourg, the name of Quidal is as common as grains of sand on the beach. This is their domain" (5) —then evokes the role oral history is to play in unearthing this story: "Rumor has it [on dit que] that they are descendants of the property of Master Antoine de Gehan-Quidal, owner of a sugar plantation" (5). ① The "on dit" or rumor provides insight into the individual experience of broader social patterns, as we learn that Gehan-Quidal's former slaves, like many others, found themselves "left behind" by abolition, literally and figuratively, as the planter returns to France and his charges are abandoned with nothing to their name but their "*kaz-neg*" cabins and the official but ineffectual status of "new citizens"—a term whose enclosure in scare quotes underlines the gap between statutory liberation and material security and mobility. Zooming in on her branch of the family name, Condé introduces her own ancestors with an evaluative judgment: "My great-grandparents were a strange bunch" (*de drôles de corps*). Yet what is strange or funny about them is deferred or contradicted by the sentences that follow, which emphasize not their distinctive traits, but instead the ordinary, typical character of their occupations, marital life, and material possessions. It is only when we learn that Oraison has a penchant for telling tales about fishing that "any qualified research specialist would describe as

① As Mary Jean Green notes, in an interview with Megan Doll, Condé states that writing this book took three years of work, and required that she interview "everybody who knew her or knew my mother or my father" in order to better understand the aspects of history that written accounts, with their focus on white colonists, leave out: "the actual facts of the people of Guadeloupe and Martinique—the way they lived, the way they suffered, the way they enjoyed life" (Doll, "An Interview with Maryse Condé"; Green, "Maryse Condé's *Victoire*", p. 305).

'erotic'" (5), that his falsetto voice makes him popular at wakes, and that his common-law wife Caldonia is a talented dream interpreter, that their individual traits begin to emerge. What makes these forebears strange is less their deviation from the norms of their time than their individuation itself and their distance from present-day modes of thinking and classification. In highlighting the perspective of the "research specialist" (specified in the French as hailing from the CNRS, a highly regarded social science institute), Condé disrupts absorptive identification, and draws attention instead to the estranged position of the present-day researcher, who labels and categorizes in an attempt to make sense of the habits of distant others.

Such markers punctuate the text throughout, calling to mind that the story we are reading is a composition stitched from various components, ranging from present-day scholarship to travelogues, newspapers, and birth and baptism records from the period, to private personal effects (notebooks, objects, and letters) and attributed and anonymous oral sources and personal communications with the author. These obtrusive notes ironically highlight an absence, as Corbin argues: "What immediately strikes the reader of Victoire is how little information is left on women of this race and class in the Guadeloupe of that era. Most live in anonymity, their deaths are hardly remarked and there is nothing left to communicate who they were after they are gone. What makes Victoire different is the daughter that she succeeded in raising and educating and, of course, the granddaughter who writes her life story."① Written traces carry only partial histories; the local society newspaper purportedly recounts Victoire's and her employer Anne-Marie Walberg's attendance at a concert, for example, but only the white, educated Anne-Marie's opinion remains accessible to history, through her personal correspondence, while Victoire's goes

① Corbin, "The Return To and Beyond the Mother", p. 235.

unrecorded (94). Victoire's celebrated culinary talents are said to be recognized in a local society magazine, which reports her menus but attributes their success and content only to "the Walbergs," never naming the cook behind the scenes.

If Condé's efforts to point out the seams linking the pieces she has brought together highlight the inaccessibility of certain aspects of Victoire's experiences and disrupt any illusion that the reader could simply substitute imagination for reality, the story itself, which occupies a major portion of the book, also seems to overflow at times the levees that modern research puts in place to mark and hold the past at a distance. Caldonia's power to interpret dreams quickly thwarts the attempt to consign it to the status of quaint ethnographic object by proving to be just as valid a mode of reading: a dream alerting her to her 14-year-old daughter Éliette's pregnancy comes true. The narrative pulls the reader into the family's thoughts and reactions, its puzzlement at Éliette's silence, and its consternation when the newborn Victoire appears with very light skin and straight, silky hair. Caldonia bonds immediately with the baby, whose young mother dies in childbirth, and this time, the author's interruption authorizes a fusion between past and present: "The child raised its eyelids and stared at Caldonia. The science of motherhood had not yet been invented, but never mind, Caldonia was deeply moved by this silent exchange" (7). Together, this process of imaginative identification and unsettlement gives Victoire, as Corbin argues, the "freedom to be opaque" without allowing that opacity to efface her: Condé's "palimpsest tales of Victoire weave the fabric/text of a life that allows the grandmother to stay imaginable but unknown in all of her singularity."① The interplay of documentation, imagination, and absence, of estrangement and empathy, endorses a particular form of representational fidelity. If restricting history to the knowable, to available

① Corbin, "The Return To and Beyond the Mother", p. 241.

documentation, and insisting on the opacity of the unknowable represents one way to be faithful to the real, empathic imagination represents another, a means for doing some justice to that which exceeds the known or which the known eclipses. *Victoire*'s juxtapositions suggest that each serves as a complement to, and check on, the other, a joining that produces not synthesis, but vacillating movement and multiplication.

Yet *Victoire* also ironizes the thirst for documentation that Condé seems not only to acknowledge but also to share, throwing into question its function in the text. The particular absence that propels Condé's investigation into Victoire's life is that of Condé's grandfather, whose identity remains unknown, Jeanne Quidal having deemed it "too painful" to discuss when the young Maryse asks her. Mary Jean Green offers a sensitive analysis of Condé's quest to elucidate this question, which leads her to the name of Dernier Argilius, a teacher and partisan of Jean-Hégésippe Légitimus, local socialist leader and later delegate to the French National Assembly. "To authenticate the reality of the oddly named Argilius," Green writes, "the narrator directs her reader to his photograph in the work of historian Sainton, whose name has already been mentioned in her text...Condé even quotes the words of an editorial penned by this heretofore unidentified grandfather in the movement's well-known newspaper, *Le Peuple*, where he pleads the cause of Guadeloupe's impoverished black population and specifically mentions the situation of black women."① Yet as Green points out, Jean-Pierre Sainton's work never mentions Argilius; the photograph is instead that of Légitimus himself, as is the quoted editorial.②

This playful, oblique paternity claim does several things. It allows

---

① Green, "Maryse Condé's *Victoire*," pp. 308 – 309.

② Ibid., p. 310. Green comments, "As Sainton describes it, 'La rhétorique dont use Légitimus est très particulière, aisément reconnaissable' (p. 214 [The rhetoric Légitimus uses is very distinctive and easily recognizable]), a line that suggests Conde's tongue-in-cheek borrowing would be easily recognizable to her educated readers in Guadeloupe" ("Maryse Condé's *Victoire*," p. 310).

Condé first, as Green notes, to offer up for consideration a question whose importance stands out in *La Belle Créole* and *La vie sans fards* as well, namely, the relationship between one's public and private actions, and the injustice we risk doing when we neglect the latter in our accounts of individuals and their role in history. Condé's critique targets figures whose public championship of the weak and marginalized contrasts hypocritically with their private exploitation of women like Victoire, impregnated and left to raise her baby alone with very few means, and whose public literacy campaign efforts and ability to harness written and spoken French for political purposes do not prevent them from neglecting illiterate creolophones, like Victoire, in their intimate lives. ① Condé's fictionalization allows her not so much to depart from reality as to condense it. The irony of disguise and indirection brings together multiple lines of thought in one character, and allows her to emphasize the value to collective history of events whose causes cannot be reduced to the idiosyncrasies of a single political figure.

Ironic archivists

The ambiguity that remains in this sly portrait of Condé's grandfather—for we cannot know if Argilius is Légitimus, or if both simply stand in for another (or perhaps multiple others fictionally condensed into one) whose

---

① Green notes, "In contrast to Conde's illiterate, creole-speaking grandmother Victoire, Légitimus, a black man of the same era, is praised by Sainton for his ability to work with the French language. Interestingly for Conde's readers, Sainton gives as an example precisely the quotation attributed to Argilius in Conde's text...In several places in her text, Conde condemns certain followers of Légitimus-her grandmother's employer Thérèse Jovial, as well as her fictitious black lover, Dernier Argilius-for failing to teach Victoire to read, implying that literacy in French might have given her an opportunity to improve her life" ("Maryse Condé's *Victoire*," p. 312).

traits they share—throws into question the value of knowing the specific identity of this progenitor. Ironic indirection prevents a clear indictment of specific individuals, but draws attention to the attitudes and actions of the readers—among whom figure the authors of the numerous "theses, monographs, and biographies" devoted to exemplary role models in the struggle against oppression (30) —who are asked to examine their own approach to history. The extension of these ironizing techniques to multiple examples throughout the text bolsters this critique. Condé whets her readers' appetite for certainty and proof with tantalizing dishes—dated private letters, multiple newspaper and magazine items, place and parish names—without ever serving a full meal. She includes accurate citations of some sources (such as a racist portrait by Anaïs Ségalas in *Récits des Antilles: le bois de la Soufrière*), but diverts a quotation from *A Parisian in Brazil* to describe Pointe-à-Pitre's Vatable canal,① gives names and editions for certain journals but omits identifying information for other texts that would facilitate verification and follow-up.② The English edition's disclaimer ("This book is largely a work of fiction. Names, characters, places, and incidents are transpositions of the life of the author's mother and grandmother"), reflecting fears of libel suits, reminds readers that a desire to protect sources might drive some of these moves, yet such a desire can hardly explain the reasons why Condé should disguise publically available sources and records or the impact this play might have on readers.

---

① Toussaint-Samson, *Une parisienne au Brésil*, 38. In Condé's citation, the word "bay" is changed to "canal," and the quote attributed to a Toussaint Chantrans (90), an evocative name that lends itself to wordplay (evoking *chantre*, or, reversing the syllables, *tranchant* or trenchant) and also recalls that of another European travel writer, Justin Girod-Chantrans (*Voyage d'un Suisse dans différentes colonies d'Amérique*).

② See, for example, Condé's partial and unattributed citations on pages 86 – 87 and 157. The print sources Condé names range from well-known catalogued and archived outlets (like the socialist publication *Le Peuple*) to more obscure sources said to have been found among Jeanne Quidal's personal belongings.

The most striking aspect of this feast of documents is perhaps their verisimilitude. If any of the titles or headlines cited are actually inventions (did a masters student at the École des Hautes Études en Sciences Sociales actually write a thesis called "From Plantation Owner to Businessman: A History of the White Creoles in Guadeloupe"? [60]), they are so close to existing publications and practice that it is both easy and difficult to infer parodic intent. The more surprising finds—such as an article from issue 51 of *L'Écho pointois* said to be found among Condé's mother's papers and to have printed the menu Victoire created for a baptism celebration—appear both plausible but also not inconceivably invented. The absence of a pattern within Condé's methods sparks curiosity, amusement, or acceptance—winks to readers rely on a particular set of reference points (or, failing that, a thirst for research), and may well go unseen by those who are less familiar with local memory, genealogies, and political figures. Yet in either case, whether or not Condé's readers fall ill of archive fever and set out to retrace her journey through libraries and interviews, what remains is something of a guerilla history: a history that imposes a version of events that is approximate but vivid and compelling. This history brings into focus the process of generalizing historical conclusions from specific examples and the elisions and omissions of the particular that occur along the way, pointing a critical finger at those traditions that exclude *Victoire*'s concerns from their purview. In proposing a menu of near certainties, plausible accounts, and clear and ambiguous inventions, Condé offers a story of what might have been, of what probably was, but also of what might have been otherwise. Attempting to confirm the "truth" or "fiction" of her references—or merely envisioning this attempt—produces an ironic doubling, a juxtaposition of textual representation against (real or imagined) extra-textual confirmation that leads not to a single truth about what happened, but to a new critical question about the interpretation of existing sources and their gaps: how does it matter that this is what happened, and how might it have happened differently?

Elmire des sept bonheurs also whets an archival appetite through the wealth of details contained in its photographs, but like Condé's text, it, too, uses ironic play to raise questions about the function of documentation and the indexical power of photography. The contrast between the humor of the tale and the somber photographic reminders of capitalism's neglected experiences—economic downturns, the devaluing of particular skills and modes of production—invites a closer look. From a different vantage point, it is the portraits, rather than the tale, which seem to be the lure here: while the volume includes one or two apparently candid shots, the large majority are meticulously composed portraits that assume a degree of self-aware participation on the part of the residents. ①The subjects of the photos gaze directly at the camera, posing their hands and sometimes offering subtle smiles. Rather than merely fragments preserved from a ruined past, these portraits also function, then, as performance. These photos are staged, and what they stage is by no means self-evident. This staging invites questioning.

If the first element that stands out in these photos is age—the age of the residents, the aging, weathered surroundings in which many of them are posed—a wealth of other details and associations crowd into these shots, which we might describe, with Guillaume Pigeard de Gurbert, as inhabited by "champs aveugles," or "blind fields," inside the photographs themselves, introducing images into the spaces typically neglected by the eye. Laguarigue subtly unsettles "the natural order of the gaze, whose normal purpose is identification," Pigeard de Gurbert argues, by creating "rambling in the gaze, fuzziness in the image, movement in the frame,

---

① In this, *Elmire des sept bonheurs* differs from Chamoiseau and Laguarigue's *Tracées de mélancholies* and *Cases en Pays-Mêlés*, which include more candid shots and frequently show people at work and in movement, sometimes acknowledging the camera's presence but often disregarding it.

and shadow in the portrait."[1] In single photos, composition lines, echoes of shapes, and mirrors giving glimpses of vistas that fall outside the camera's direct line of sight trope the "scene" ironically, turning what the eye's "natural" habit might mistake for a univocal and unequivocal signifier, coincident with its signified, into a series of layered meanings that cannot merely be identified, but must be read. Spanning multiple photos, repeated objects and patterns build themes that echo and enter into tension with one another. Clocks and crosses dominate these photos, appearing frequently among the objects pictured in the background, but also as a compositional structure. The placement of family photos, decorative objects, and television sets visually reproduce the circles formed by the clocks which occupy the center of several of these portraits,[2] while residents' bodies, along with the vertical and horizontal lines of doorframes, windowsills, shelves, and shadows, form crosses echoing, in secular terms, the crucifixes and icons that decorate the interior.

The portrait of Faustin Hébert, whose seeming emptiness would seem to contrast with the teeming interiors of the preceding panels, shows this ironic play of meaning well. The shallow focus and medium shot draw attention to Hébert, who is pictured slightly left of center and occupies most

---

① Pigeard de Gurbert, "Les champs aveugles." My translation. Pigeard de Gurbert explains that he borrows the term from Pascal Bonitzer, who uses it to describe fields that fall outside of cinematic shots, but applies it differently to highlight components of the image that go unseen only through habit and inattention.

② See, for example, the photos of Thérèse and Roland Clémentine, and Nanette and Gesner Germany, which are arranged on facing pages in the French edition (pp. 24 – 25) and whose compositional departures from one another only better highlight each one's symmetry and spark curiosity. In each, a wall clock hangs at a central focal point, and decorative objects form frames around the timepiece. The Clémentine's trio of family photos echoes the trinity evoked by a Madonna and child, and a painting of Christ, while a television set and electric fan form a mundane mirror for the religious icons. Breaks in symmetry (a blurry photo of a group of children on one side, and a picture of a German shepherd, on the other), however, caution against over-reading these parallels.

of the frame. Hébert looks directly and knowingly at the camera, his face turned very slightly away, as if to give the viewer a better glimpse of the straw hat behind his shoulder, the only decoration on a bare, concrete wall. The stone background is sparse yet richly textured; the straw hat hangs at the center of a cross formed by cracks and shadows in the wall, lending an aura of respect and somewhat playful sanctity to this figure, his work, and the testimony he has contributed. This playful worship is repeated throughout the images, as in the verbal tale, which reminds readers, on the page facing Hébert's portrait, that this woman that is Elmira, this "mama, matador, saint, haughty, marvelous, a tabernacle of hungry lives," does not just appear to anyone, that "you had to deserve her, according to rules our lawbooks and apocryphal bibles did not recognize" (35, 22, translation modified).

If compositional considerations such as this highlight the photographer's role and skill—the repetition of techniques building an impression of authorial purpose and thematic development—other choices draw attention back to limits of authorial control and the life that escapes photography's frames. Lucien Irilo's burning cigarette waits, immobile, for the hand to pick it up; his glasses reflect a glare that partially obscures his eyes, reminding us of our lack of access to his own thoughts and vision. Clothilde and Emmanuel Billard sit on either side of a doily-covered television set tuned to a cartoon featuring an incongruous, angry gorilla; the stilled cartoon, the mirror above that reflects the scene from a different angle, and the pair of clocks resting on a sideboard, each telling different times, call attention to the photographer's aspiration and failure to capture time, which can only be frozen in frames, beyond which life continues to follow its course.

It is perhaps the repeated image of holding one's face in one's hands, however, that raises the most significant questions about the goals and effects of the project to which these Gros-Morne residents have lent their likenesses. This gesture occurs in the portrait of Renoir Ovarbury (featured both in the text and on the cover), in the portrait of Joachim-Belisaire Vesanes, and in the portrait of Apolline Mexique, who raises one hand to her chin and holds the other across her body. ①Evoking contemplation and a degree of active participation, this gesture stages both self-awareness and absorption. Viewed in isolation, each portrait seems to reflect and elicit serious thought, even sorrow or fatigue; yet as it repeats over different pages, the gesture begins to appear less and less spontaneous, and more and more fanciful or ironic. Drawing attention to the embodiment and circulation of visual representation, this gesture is both repeated and altered in its reproduction, prompting us to look more closely into the cultural and material economies in which this project was conceived and marketed.

The book itself provides a number of pieces of information that help us examine this question. It is jointly copyrighted by Gallimard, a major French press, and the Saint-Étienne Distillery itself, whose co-owner, film director Florette Hayot, is credited by the editorial staff (in the French version), with conceiving the project. Saint-Étienne is one of Martinique's nine distilleries, located on a very old property that was converted from sugar to rum production in 1883. In 1994, it was purchased in a state of decline by its current owners, José and Florette Hayot, who, like the photographer Laguarigue, belong to the minority *béké* planter class. The co-owners have since sought to make of Saint-Étienne not only a productive distillery, but also to restore its architecture and transform it into a historical monument and cultural center. The site now houses a performance space inspired by poet and theorist Édouard Glissant, and a permanent

---

① Laguarigue has used some of these portraits in collages featured at the Habitation Saint-Étienne's exhibit space. See also his main website (available in both French and English), which contains a number of samples, including a reproduction of the portrait of Apolline Mexique: http://www.delaguarigue.com.

photographic exhibit by Laguarigue, into which many of the Elmira works have been integrated in new forms. Glissant himself participated in dedication ceremonies there, and the center has also held events celebrating Chamoiseau's work, among others. ①

Seen as part of the plantation's efforts to promote cultural memory, *Elmire des sept bonheurs* takes on the status of an economic and cultural intervention in a society in which rum, and the plantation sites that produce rum, occupy a curious place. The plantation is at once the cradle of Creole identity, the site where various languages and ethnic affiliations came together to form a society, and at the same time the generator of persistent cleavages and social tensions within this shared Creoleness. In an economic age where local production of any sort has dwindled, and the Martinican economy depends heavily on State subsidies and employment, rum takes on a privileged status as a symbol of Martinican identity, of past and potentially future productivity. Saint-Étienne co-owner José Hayot has asserted that, "Rum is the only Martinican product that is a cultural product; rum is truly the *terroir*, the history of Martinique with all its pain and suffering. It's a product of hope, too, because Martinican society, which is a composite, Creole society, is a society of the future, and today, to be Creole is to be from the whole world, one can be from everywhere. Rum carries the somewhat universal cultural message of this Creoleness.... "②

Such a view may serve the commercial interests of the owners in creating a global market for the product, but this interest does not exhaust its impact. Within a local context, to tie rum explicitly to the pain and suffering of the past, to foreground the promotion of historical memory, and to hitch the distillery's success to a demand for local cultural production

---

① For more on the Habitation Saint-Étienne's exhibit space, Les Foudres HSE, see the page devoted to it on the distillery's website: http: //www. rhumhse. com/art/foudres/.

② Marly, "Monsieur José Hayot", my translation.

is to take a particular stance that represents a break with the white, planter class's traditional avoidance or denial of this history and denial of its own implication in oppressive economic structures. ① It also represents a very deliberate attempt at crossing entrenched class divisions, at creating opportunities for collaborative cultural production. ② Without suggesting that this sort of patronage of memory and the arts is a satisfactory solution to all conflicts over land use, unequal distribution of wealth, and *béké* planter monopolies in Martinique, keeping these particulars in mind—and recalling that collaborations across social boundaries still draw suspicion and critique, and cannot simply be taken for granted③—can usefully inflect how we might read Elmira's stagings, and the curious forms of reflexivity it seems to demand.

In the acknowledgements at the start of the book, Chamoiseau attributes a sort of collective authorship to the residents of Gros-Morne, thanking these "commanders of memory" for "their willingness to share

---

① *Béké* industrial leader Alain Huyghues Despointes drew outrage, for example, when he commented in a documentary televised February 6, 2009 by Canal + (*Les derniers maîtres de la Martinique*) that he was against miscegenation and that historians were wrong to focus only on the bad sides of colonialism and to ignore its benefits. José Hayot and Jean-Luc de Laguarigue both publically condemned Huyghues Despointes remarks. See Hayot, "Antilles: contre l'obscurité" and Laguarigue, "Communiqué".

② *Tracées de mélancolies*, published a year later, shows signs of this shift in that it is no longer co-published with Gallimard, but by the Habitation Saint-Étienne alone, supported by funding from La DRAC Martinique (Direction régionale des affaires culturelles de Martinique, a branch of France's Ministry of Culture, renamed Direction des affaires culturelles or DAC in 2011), and advance purchases made by other distilleries (Dillon, Depaz, Fondation Clément) and a number of other local firms and industries.

③ As Wendy Knepper recalls in her discussion of Chamoiseau's contributions to the Martinican film industry, working with José Hayot on the production of the film *Nord Plage* "proved to be a controversial choice for Chamoiseau because some criticized his decision to collaborate with a *béké*" (*Patrick Chamoiseau*, p. 189). See also Simek, *Hunger and Irony in the French Caribbean: Literature, Theory, and Public Life*, chapter five, for a discussion of Maryse Condé's collaboration with *béké* industrial leader Amédée Huyghues Despointes and the negative responses she received.

their testimony with us" (5) (Remerciements à ces habitants du Gros-Morne, commandeurs des souvenirs, qui ont bien voulu nous porter témoignage [4]).[①] If we consider these residents as contributors or informants engaging with the photographer and the viewer rather than as passive objects caught unawares by the camera, their portraits function somewhat otherwise than as documents conveying a particular historical content—or documents in need of a spokesperson—and more like a form of signature. To read these photos as somber and poignant—or rather as *only* somber and poignant—is perhaps to mistake this act of signing, or co-signing on the part of the subjects for a documentary impulse on the part of the photographer.

We cannot of course infer from the photos themselves, which have been widely diffused beyond their point of production, that the residents featured in the published text were aware of the contours of Laguarigue and Chamoiseau's project at the time they were photographed, particularly since many of these images have been used in other exhibits (including the permanent exhibit at the Habitation Saint-Étienne) and were not designed exclusively for *Elmire des sept bonheurs*. Yet it is important to recall that these images circulate locally, that the Chamoiseau and Laguarigue live and work in Martinique, and that they participate regularly in events held at the Habitation Saint-Étienne in Gros-Morne (a small town with a population of just over 10, 000), with an audience likely to include neighbors, friends, and acquaintances of the people who sat for these photographs, as well as some of the "subjects" themselves. These conditions certainly impact not only local viewers' experiences and reactions, but also the authors' awareness of their work's reception and implication in local, communal dialogues.

Among these dialogues figures Habitation Saint-Étienne's broader effort

---

① Translation modified.

"to constitute (at all levels of thought, imagination, celebration, sharing, pleasure, and thus beauty) everything we're missing today and that makes living better," and to do this cultural work in a space open to the public, for the public. ①In its collaborative or communal dimensions, *Elmire des sept bonheurs* launches and participates in this mission. The 2010 opening of Les Foudres, a multifunctional meeting space at the Habitation Saint-Étienne that hosts a range of conferences, films, concerts, and exhibits, concretized this mission to provide a public forum, free of charge, for events appealing to various audiences. Describing Les Foudres' philosophy, Guillaume Pigeard de Gurbert asserts, "Thinking or dreaming for oneself does not mean thinking or dreaming by oneself, alone, but on the contrary, thinking and imagining together with others.... Hence Les Foudres HSE develops culture in a number of public spaces, culture being not a private possession but a public matter par excellence, which is to say the business of the people."②

In enlisting local residents in this project, and in the creation of this tongue-in-cheek tale, the text asserts the value of ironic play in the strong sense of playful, affective engagement. In so doing, it invites us not so much to distance ourselves from the projection of desire that is Elmira, but to traverse the separation of subject and object underpinning efforts at cognitive distancing and melancholic capture that the ruin habitually inspires. At the end of his tale, the narrator comes to such an

---

① My translation. This mission statement or testimony ("Une culture d'émotions"), on HSE Les Foudres' website, is credited to Patrick Chamoiseau. The French reads, "Les Foudres HSE doivent constituer (à tous les niveaux de la pensée, de l'imaginaire, de la fête, du partage, du plaisir, et donc de la beauté) tout ce qui aujourd'hui nous manque et qui rend mieux vivant."

② Pigeard de Gurbert, "Un esprit de différence." My translation. The French reads, "Penser ou rêver par soi-même ne veut pas dire penser ou rêver tout seul, mais au contraire penser et imaginer en commun avec d'autres.... Ce pourquoi les Foudres HSE déclinent la culture en de multiples espaces publics, la culture n'étant pas un bien privé mais la chose publique par excellence, c'est-à-dire la chose du peuple."

understanding, concluding that what he eventually learned was that:

> Elmira was in each of us, between the conscious and the unconscious, where the maps of flesh and spirit come together to suggest to each of us the *impossibility* of our lives, its trace of elevation, the star of plenitude by which we set our art, our voice, every gesture of our existence. We are all children in that regard. Gros-Morne lifts the richness of its soil above our ruined dreams. The distillery stands here, smoking out its challenges and rising up to them as it has for so many years. In our difficult wait, among the embers of hope and disenchantment that guide our will, we endeavor, in moderation, to live as best we can; and, as Elmira suggests, we try—with difficult desires, at the highest degree of impossibility—to find our quiet happiness. (pp. 29 –30, translation modified)

Elmira becomes an internal muse, a source of creative surpassing or ironic enchantment that hinges on a capacity for play, for an alternative rationality that sets into productive tension the hermeneutics of faith and suspicion and the varying affective responses they involve. In an important sense, *Elmire*'s photographs ironically authorize, rather than puncture, the whimsy of the written story, inviting us to take the story seriously, to join in the celebration of Elmira, and the pleasures of creative play.

Living Irony in the Post-Colony

Through ironic enchantment, Elmira passes from mere laughable delusion or melancholic ruin to utopian vision, and the co-signed text takes on the dimensions of a stage in a much more literal sense: a stage on which new creative imaginations and relations of cultural production can be given space to unfold. An inaugural text of sorts, *Elmire des sept bonheurs* displays the important mediating role the photographer, the writer, and the patron—those with access to economic and cultural capital—play in initiating and sustaining these new modes of production and relation. As a product of artistic and editorial care and financial resources, the textembodies traces of the material barriers its creators seek to unsettle. If *Elmire* makes area residents and distillery workers participants in the project to reform cultural and economic relationships, it does so by working within the language of the dominant discourse, turning that language to different ends.

Victoire, les saveurs et les mots also takes on the task of reimagining relations of cultural production, and similarly critiques social hierarchies, foregrounding the educated, renowned author's role in making a place for excluded forms of creativity. Throughout the book, Condé develops the idea that cooking and writing are both creative acts, worthy of appreciation and memory. "What I am claiming," writes Condé at the moment at which Victoire becomes a cook for the Walberg family, "is the legacy of this woman, who apparently did not leave any. I want to establish the link between her creativity and mine, to switch from the savors, the colors, and the smells of meat and vegetables to those of words" (59). Cooking, for Victoire, involves not only preparing and executing meals, but inventing, losing herself in the absorbing task of composing dishes, "like a writer hunched over her computer" (59). For Victoire, who has trouble expressing herself verbally, to cook is to communicate, to give a gift, and to show love—and her daughter Jeanne's picky eating habits become a way for her child to rebel against her.

If Jeanne regards her mother as exploited by the Walbergs—for her labor and, as Boniface Walberg's mistress, for her body—Victoire, Condé imagines, sees her employers as benefactors, or at least as non-enemies, having known no other life than that of a live-in servant, with no wages or possessions to her name. If Jeanne manages to impose her views and separate her mother from the Walbergs once she becomes employed as a teacher and able to support her mother on her own, Victoire reasserts her perspective at the end of her life. Dying of cancer, she prevails on Jeanne to invite the Walberg family to a final dinner with Jeanne and her husband, an event Condé describes in detail:

> I am going to call this meal "The Last Supper." It could be the subject of a painting with Victoire in the center, surrounded by the people she had cherished throughout her life. But on that particular day, she did not simply reunite those who were dear to her before death carried her off. It was her way of writing her last will and testament. One day, she hoped, color would no longer be an evil spell. One day, Guadeloupe would no longer be tortured by questions of class.... Both [white Creoles and Grands Nègres] would get along, freely intermingle, and who knows, love each other. (189)

Giving this event the title of one of the most famous, debated, and speculation-provoking works of art in the Western tradition creates two audacious parallels, between Condé and the genius painter, and between Victoire and Christ. In imbuing this scene with heroism while affiliating herself with an artist read popularly today as a master of subtlety and ambiguity, Condé seems to push the limits of verisimilitude, ironizing her own re-creation of Victoire's mindset. In the following pages, Condé goes on to doubt her mother's own heroic portrait of Victoire's last words— " '*Sé douvan zot kalé à pwézan. Mwen pé pati.*' (You go on. I can leave now.)" —as improbable, arguing that pain and remorse led Jeanne to mythologize Victoire's death when, more likely, she slipped away quietly under the effects of heavy doses of morphine (194). Irony warns against the tendency to read the past as we would prefer it have been, and puts a check on the relief brought by myth-making.

At the same time, "The Last Supper" describes Victoire quite realistically as a woman in pain, betrayed by the social conditions of her time, and unable to enjoy for herself the fruits of her sacrifices. From this perspective, the "Ultima Cena" comes to represent not a myth to deflate, but a "prophetic vision of the past," one that makes the past speak falsely, ironically, in order to tell truths. Playing on her own reputation as "inconvenante"① —improper, difficult to classify, and provocative—Condé positions herself through this portrait as Victoire's ironic disciple, heir to a "secretive, enigmatic" woman, the "improper architect (architecte inconvenante) of a liberation that we, her descendants, have known how to enjoy to the full" (195). Bold impropriety brings emancipation, and Condé's own "improper" reading of Victoire's intentions translates Victoire's creative language into modern terms, a faithful betrayal that makes Victoire's efforts legible and impactful in the present. In so doing, Condé's irony turns these terms back upon themselves, questioning the grounds on which Victoire's creativity is deemed illegible or illiterate. If *Elmire des sept bonheurs* democratizes culture by displaying the capacity for irony shared across social divides, *Victoire, les saveurs et les mots* insists on the irreducible tensions that inhabit sociability, daring readers to accommodate these differences and take up Victoire's inconvenient legacy themselves.

Works Cited:

1. Britton, Celia. *Language and Literary Form in French Caribbean Writing.* Contemporary French and Francophone Cultures, 31. Liverpool: Liverpool University Press, 2014.

2. Catinchi, Philippe Jean. "Livraisons." *Le Monde.* April 24, 1998. Lexis Nexis Academic.

---

① Cottenet-Hage and Moudileno, *Maryse Condé: Une nomade inconvenante.*

3. Chamoiseau, Patrick. *Un dimanche au cachot*. Paris: Gallimard, 2007.

4. Chamoiseau, Patrick and Jean-Luc de Laguarigue. *Cases en Pays-Mêlés*. Habitation Saint-Étienne: Éditions Traces HSE, 2000.

——. *Elmire des sept bonheurs: Confidences d'un vieux travailleur de la distillerie Saint-Étienne*. Paris: Sonofa-Habitation Saint-Étienne and Éditions Gallimard, 1998.

——. *Seven Dreams of Elmira: A Tale of Martinique. Being the Confessions of an Old Worker at the Saint-Etienne Distillery*. Translated by Mark Polizzotti. Cambridge, Massachusetts: Zoland Books, 1999.

——. *Tracées de melancholies*. Habitation Saint-Étienne: Éditions Traces HSE, 1999.

5. Condé, Maryse. *Victoire, les saveurs et les mots*. Paris: Mercure de France, 2006.

——. *Victoire, My Mother's Mother*. Translated by Richard Philcox. New York: Atria, 2010.

6. Cottenet-Hage, Madeleine and Lydie Moudileno, eds. *Maryse Condé: Une nomade inconvenante*. Paris: Ibis Rouge Editions, 2002.

7. Corbin, Laurie. "The Return to and Beyond the Mother: Maryse Condé and Representations of Maternity." *Life Writing*. 4, 2 (2007): 231-45.

8. Doll, Megan. "An Interview with Maryse Condé." http://www.bookslut.com/features/2010_02_015665.php.

9. Glissant, Édouard. *Caribbean Discourse: Selected Essays*. Translated by Michael Dash. CARAF Books. Charlottesville: University Press of Virginia, 1989.

10. Green, Mary Jean. "Maryse Condé's *Victoire*: Thinking Back through Her Mothers." *Nottingham French Studies*, 53.3 (2014): 297-313.

11. Habitation Saint-Étienne. "Les Foudres HSE" website. http://art.habitation-saint-etienne.com/foudres/.

12. Hayot, José. "Antilles: contre l'obscurité." Mediapart. February 20, 2009. Blog. https://blogs.mediapart.fr/edition/les-invites-de-mediapart/article/200209/antilles-contre-l-obscurite-par-jose-hayot.

13. Kirkus Reviews. "Seven Dreams of Elmira: A Tale of Martinique." August 1, 1999. Posted online May 20, 2010. https://www.kirkusreviews.com/book-reviews/patrick-chamoiseau/seven-dreams-of-elmira/.

14. Knepper, Wendy. *Patrick Chamoiseau: A Critical Introduction*. Jackson: University Press of Mississippi. 2012.

15. Kwateh, A. "Elmire au bonheur des hommes." *Antilla* 773 (March 27, 1998). http://

habitation-saint-etienne. com/ art/ wp-content/ uploads/2012/01/ Elmire-Antilla. jpg.

16. Laguarigue, Jean-Luc de. "Communiqué." Gens de Pays. Blog. http: //gensdepays. blogspot. com/2009_ 02_ 01_ archive. html.

——. "Un autre monde." *Gens de pays*. Blog. http: //gensdepays. blogspot. com/ search/label/Bio.

——. "Jean-Luc de Laguarigue. Photographe de la Caraïbe." Artist's website. http: // www. delaguarigue. com.

17. Landy, Joshua A. and Michael Saler, eds. *The Re-enchantment of the World: Secular Magic in a Rational Age* (Stanford: Stanford UP, 2009).

18. Marly, Virginie. "Monsieur José Hayot, Propriétaire de la Rhumerie l'Habitation Saint-Etienne en Martinique-Vinexpo 2005." *Lettre vinomedia* 162 (June 27, 2005). http: //www. vin-events. com/lettre-vinomedia/ archives/162/1 _ b3ea025d – 872d – 4426 – 863a – cd2d09e8aacd. asp? id_ rubrique = 1&rubrique = Les + interviews&dir = interviews&requete = &phrase = 0&datecreation = undefined&absolutePage = 1.

19. Moudileno, Lydie. "Archéologie du cachot," *Présence francophone* 81 (2014): 48 – 63.

20. Pigeard de Gurbert, Guillaume. "Les champs aveugles." In Jean-Luc de Laguarigue. *Gens de pays*. January 31, 2007. Blog. http: //gensdepays. blogspot. com/2007/ 01/champs-aveugles. html.

21. Saler, Michael. "Modernity, Disenchantment, and the Ironic Imagination." *Philosophy and Literature*. 28. 1 (2004): 137 – 149.

22. Simek, Nicole. *Hunger and Irony in the French Caribbean: Literature, Theory, and Public Life*. New York: Palgrave Macmillan, 2016.

23. Steinberg, Sybil. "Forecasts: Fiction," *Publishers Weekly*. 246, 30 (1999): 69. Business Source Premier.

24. Toussaint-Samson, Adèle. *Une parisienne au Brésil*. Paris: Paul Ollendorff, 1883. Gallica, Bibliothèque Nationale de France. http: //gallica. bnf. fr/ark: / 12148/bpt6k5747774p.

25. Walcott, Derek. "Nobel Lecture: The Antilles: Fragments of Epic Memory." *Nobelprize. org*. Nobel Media AB 2013. Feb 2, 2014. http: //www. nobelprize. org/nobel_ prizes/literature/laureates/1992/walcott-lecture. html.

——. "The Royal Palms" *The London Magazine*. 1. 11 (1962): 12 – 13.

Unification, Fit-in, and Diaspora: An Ecocritical Analysis of Representation of the Position of Humanity in Chinese Literature

SONG Lili*

中文摘要　生态批评作为一种批评视角进入越来越广阔的文本视域，产生越来越大的跨学科活力，释放出让所有的文学加入到合力思考人与自然关系的潜能。中国文学也不例外。在研究人类文化与物质自然的关系的时候，对于人类处于何种位置及由此生发的态度在研究中具有重要的意义。本文将选取中国文学中不同阶段的文本，即《庄子》、陶渊明的田园之歌以及现代环境作家徐刚、郭雪博的作品进行生态批评视角的分析解读，试图追踪文本中对人类在自然世界中的位置的再现与思考。分析发现三个不同时期的作品所展现的人与自然世界的关系分别是合一、适应与离散，所展现的人类的位置的思考是不同的：分别是庄子的如何保持与自然合一的位置、陶渊明的努力回归适应自然的存在以及现代环境写作所再现的逐渐自我放逐、离开故有家园的离散之境。

* 宋丽丽，比较文学博士，清华大学外文系副教授，美国环境与文学协会会员。主要研究方向为生态批评与环境文学，比较文学与世界文学。

关键词 生态批评；人类位置；合一；适应；离散

Ecocriticism, the study of "relationship between literature and physical environment" has gathered its scattered literary energy since the second half of 20th century first in the United States and then in the rest of the world, and has been revealing an immensehorizon and compatibility to examine human position in the earth existing system. Tracing Buell's study alone from *The Environmental Imagination* (1995) to his *Writing for the Endangered World* (2001), and to *The Future of Environmental Criticism* (2005), we can see that the research of the literary texts are gaining a wider coverage which is not only focusing on the environmental writings or the natural writings like the Thoreauian canons, but also drawing attention to the other genres and canonical works, such as works by Dresser and Faulkner etc to picture up the human position. Moreover while the study of ecocriticism bears on the inclusiveness of texts; it also opens to the transcultural and interdisciplinary dimension on the offset. ASLE (Association for the Study of Literature and Environment) has developed branches, which is a conglomerate of the local study of ecocriticism, such as Japan, Korea, Britain, Australia, New Zealand, Germany etc. As Scott Slovic put it *In ISLE Reader Ecocrticism*, 1993 – 2003 (2003), "the ecocritical bailiwick includes not only the study of the explicit treatment of human-nonhuman relationships in literature, but also the reading of any work of literature (in any genre) in an effort to discern its environment implications. We believe that every literary work can be read from a "green" perspective, and that linguistic, conceptual, and analytical frameworks developed in any non literary discipline may be incorporated into an ecocritical reading." (ISLE Reader, xix) To associate the profession of literary study with the practical matter of life or death environmental issues which is the basic and the essential drive of ecocriticism serves as a common ground for the study of any literature anywhere. Thus ecocriticism is a very practical perspective or inlet into literary texts to reflect the position and function of humanity in relation to what is happening in the natural environment.

With the fast spreading of the dimension of ecocriticism, it has developed several various methodological and thematic academic route by pastoralism (D. Worster, L. Marx, R. Williams, L. Buell,) narrative scholarship (S. Slavic), literary ecology (J. Meeker), literature of place (D. N. Dresse), romantic literary ecology (J. Bate, K. Kroaber) etc. Reflecting upon these conceptual focuses, we will come upon the same backbone emerged out of each of the route: the pondering of the position of humanity, which drives us back to Thoreau's fundamental question "where we lived and what we lived for?" Since "We" assumed the role of talking, and we were to bear on the responsibility of environmental and ecological protection, where we had, could, and should situate us would be the key question to ask.

Thus we can say the questioning the position of humanity is the latent fundamental motivation of ecocriticism or environmental criticism①. When Glotfelty assured the term, ecocriticism, she mentioned the decisive role of positional thinking and said: " they favor eco-over enviro-because, analogous to the science of ecology, ecocriticism studies relationships between things, in this case, between human culture and the physical world. Furthermore, in its connotations, enviro-is anthropocentric and dualistic, implying that we humans are at the centre, surrounded by everything that is not us, environment. Eco-, in contrast, implies interdependent communities, integrated systems, and strong connections

① The differences between ecocriticism and environmental criticism is quite ambiguous, though different critics tend to favor one term over another, see Buell as an example, he prefers environmental criticism to ecocriticism. But he never distinct the two term independent of one another. So I use "or" to mean I take the two term at the same time with regard to the common environmental concern.

among constituent parts ... . " (Ecocriticism Reader, xx) When the relationship between human cultural and the physical world is studied, the position of human beings and the attitude from that position are to play an important role in the effect of the study. It is not just a matter of term to be applied, it will indicate the valorization of the critical discourse. Actually, it is not eco-or enviro-that matters, or rather it is the where and who human beings are that decides the way to approach the relationship. Joseph Meeker poked the sense of the position of humanity in his *The Comedy of Survival*: *Studies in Literary Ecology* (1974): "Human values could no longer be based on the assumption that man is alone at the centre of creation; ... Ecology challenges mankind to vigorous complexity, not passive simplicity". (Meeker, 39) Ecology is about the complex interrelated relationship between organism and inorganism. Ecologist informed us the critical ecological situation we are facing and the destructions that human beings inflicted upon the nature world. But they haven't ever told the answer to the question by the numbers they observed from nature where and whom human beings are. Literature, as an aesthetic expression and representation of human action and human relations to other beings, plays the function of a certain mirror against which we could possibly find the representation of his whereabouts and thus if the literary study were to take into account the intricate relationships within and among literary works, the study of human position could serves as an access to the vigorous complexity of comprehending human position beyond the anthropocentric mindset in the living system of earth ecology.

But how? Buell made the first attempt in which he studied the "capacity of environmental texts to model ecocentric thinking" in his first book *The Environmental Imagination*, by promoting the aesthetics of relinquishment. He said: "The aesthetics of relinquishment implied rather, suspension of ego, to the point of feeling the environment to be at least as worthy of attention as oneself and of experiencing oneself as situated among many interacting presences." (Buell, 178) Buell's assumption of situating oneself among many interacting presences reminds us to question the positional evolution of the ego and affective relation of ego in the environment or rather the real state of existence.

This has been deeply imbedded in the human culture and leads to the thinking of ontological implication by locating the answer to whom and where we were, are and would be with regard to the physical environment in the representation of literature. The ecological survey of the position of humanity has a sweeping revolutionary significance. It could be expressed by Reich's words in his *The Greening of America*: "Its ultimate creation will be a new and enduring wholeness and beauty—a renewed relationship of man to himself, to other man, to society, to nature, and to the land." (Reich, 2) The implication is subject to be associated with searching for the truth of human position in the vast ecosystem. The truth of human position which is to be examined in relation to the physical natural beings inevitably casts fundamental reinvestigation in three interrelated levels of thinking: the belief, the ethic, and the aesthetic. It indicates a process of going from the broken fragments to the whole, and grasping the holistic view of human position with a joint effort of the three levels of speculation. It would necessarily take some traveling from global to local, from past to present through literature texts which presumably represent the holistic reality of relationship between human being and the physical environment. This paper will make such a journey to Chinese literature by stopping at three texts from different historical times.

In China, the relationship between literature and environment is both an old story and new one. It is old story in that until the down of modern time, literature had been considered the recreation of the nature's way and speaking for the minds of sky and earth as stated in Liuxie's Wenxindiaolong. The theme of pondering human position in the nature world has propped up the body of traditional Chinese literature since

Zhuangzi. It is a new story in that literature emerged again as a mirror to reflect the deteriorating reality of nature environment and the destructive reality afflicted with human behaviour. Chinese Association of Environment and Culture, which was established in 1991, mainly composed of environmental oriented writers is striving to promote the environmental consciousness at least among the writers who are expected to serve as igniters for the development of environmental literature and culture. A group of environmental oriented writers like literary reporter, Xu Gang, Mongolian fiction writer, Guo Xuebo and the ecological novelist, Zhe Fu etc. , have devoted themselves to hold up the banner of writing for the environmental protection and have deeply exposed and represented the environmental situation in contemporary China. Three "Green" anthologies consisting of 9 books of green novels and literary reports, as well as essays were published. Journals like *Journal of Poyang Lake* and *Green Leaves*, etc. are dedicated to publish green creative and academic writings. In the Chinese academic field, in spite of the differences in terminology such as ecoaesthetic, ecological literary theory etc. , more and more Chinese literary scholars showed their research interest in the direction of the environmental and ecological consideration by reexamining Chinese literary theory, discussing ecological being, reexamining Tao's tradition, searching ecosophy from Chinese philosophy. Some Ph. D. students from Universities like Beijing Languages and Culture University, Shandong University, Suzhou University etc. are taking ecocriticism as their dissertation focus.

So far, to be sure, the possibility of connecting the fast development of world ecocriticism with the concerned study and contribution of Chinese literature lies in the fact that part of Chinese literary history which has taken the relationship of man and nature as its main aesthetic focus ranging from the earliest natural writer and philosopher, Zhuangzi (369-286 B. C), the founder of Chinese pastoral poems, Tao Yuanming (365 – 427) and the contemporary environmental writers, corresponds well to the environmental consideration of literature representation as a source to "redirect human consciousness to a full consideration of its place in a threatened natural world". (Ecocriticism Reader: 237) It is inspirational to make an ecocritical survey of Chinese literature which consists in a potential knowledge of the relationship between man and nature both in literary resources and in the production of the environmental thinking, particularly about human position. In other words, insomuch as literary study of the relationship between human beings and the physical environment has been pushed under the spotlight, it is inevitable and important to make an ecocritical travel through the long history of Chinese literature. This paper will deal with three texts, Zhuangzi, Tao Yuanming and Xu Gang with time difference of about one thousand years apart.

Talking about the historical advantage of Chinese literature, there is one theme which had penetrated the representation of Chinese literature both ancient and present, that is, the representation of the pondering of human position in this world. From earliest zhuangzi (369 – 286BC), by way of pastoral poets like Tao Yuanming (365 – 427), to the present environmental writers like Xu Gang (1945—) and Guo Xuebo (1948—), Chinese literature offers principle resources in the representation of the pondering of ecological evolution of the man and nature relationship. The pondering of the human position in this world is closely connected with ecological and environmental concern by virtue of governing one's behavioron the basis of knowing oneself in the ecosystem. Through analysis of the texts, the paper discovers that the evolution of thinking on human position related to nature appears to undergo three stages: one is the stage of unification, in which human beings had been thought as one unified and inseparable part of nature; the second one is the stage of fit-in in which human had been thought as guests whose most important position is to fit into holistic structure of the world; the third one is the stage of diaspora in which human beings consider themselves as the dominator and exploiter of the world, but ironically they are losing their balanced ecological home to an instable and insecure future by their insatiable consumption.

Unification

On the dimension of ecocritical study in the Chinese context, Zhuangzi (369 – 286B. C.) was probably an important and original place to start for combing the representation of man and nature relationship. Zhuangzi was a Chinese philosopher and writer in warring period with a rich metaecological thinking concerning position of humanity. The book that he left to us with the same name *Zhuangzi* containing about 33 passages in the most up-to-date version, along with *Zhouyi*, and *Laozi*, were considered "Three Mysteries". The heart of Zhuangzi's view of man and nature relationship is unification, that is, oneness in his word. In his most important passage titled Qiwulun (on equalization), he put forward the most important assertion that "Heaven, earth and I exists at the same time, all the natural things and I are in oneness" (Zhuang Zi, 29)① In this assertion, there lies three important terms, "oneness", "I", "natural things". The underlined motivation of making such an assertion arose from the pondering of position with regard to the relationship with the physical natural beings, in the contemporary term, the ecosystem.

In oneness, Zhuanzi situated himself among the natural things by unification. This can be proved by the following story:

> Nanguo Ziqi sat leaning on his low table. He gazed at the sky and breathed gently, in a trance as if his soul had left his body. His disciple

① In this paper I use "oneness" to replace the "uniformity" in Wang's translation.

Yancheng Ziyou, who stood in waiting before him, said, "How does it come to this? Can your body really become thus like a withered tree and your soul like dead ashes? Your appearance as you lean on your low table today is not the same as it used to be."

Ziqi said, "Yan, you've asked a good question. Do you know that I lost myself? You have heard the music of the man, but you haven't heard the music of the earth. You may have heard the music of the earth, but you may not have heard the music of the heaven!"

...

Ziyi said, "the music of the earth is the sound of from all those hollows while the music of the man is the sound from different flutes and pipes."

Ziqi said the music of the heaven is varied, but it is the same wind that makes different hollows produce different sounds. Each hollow produces its own sound; what else is there to emit the sound? (15 – 17)

Here, in the first place, Zhuangzi supposed that the natural world was a live body while human body was just subject to the rythm of the movement of natural body. The ideal existence would be in tune with everything when they were themselves. There is no denying that the speculation of being united with the nature grounded on the belief in the metaphysical harmony of oneness with everything that was properly situated in his place. The relationship between human and everything in nature was far from being connected together, rather it was a unified oneness of various individuals, being oneness means being oneself as an individual in the relationship with everything else. Oneness means the whole of being when each being remained its special being. The extreme condition for being oneness was that nothing was manipulating and dominating over anything else and there was no bother between one another. Once the manipulating and domination was applied, the oneness would tend to break. The intactness of oneness would come to be toppled and the unification would break apart. Harmonious sound would fade away and be replaced by noise and disturbance. This belief corresponds with the ecological concept of food chain which is a natural interrelated relationship. One of the differences between Zhuangzi's oneness and the ecological concept of food chain is that human being was ideally supposed to be himself in the oneness while in food chain human position is controversially uncertain. The problem in Zhuangzi's oneness which modern people would not put up with was that it minimized the material being of human being while the spiritual being was so much stressed. Paradoxically this problem was exactly the answer that modern people was searching for in protecting themselves and the endangered earth from the ecological and environmental crisis. Annie Dillard, a contemporary American environmental writer, coincided with Zhuangzi's speculation of human position in her effort of retracing human position in the nature with regard to the weasel's existence. "But I might learn something of mindlessness, something of the purity of living in the physical sense and the dignity of living without bias or motive. ...I would like to live as I should, as the weasel lives as he should." (Anderson, 110) However in Annie Dillard, we feel a much stronger wish, a wish to know oneself, a wish to go back to the very beginning of the relationship with nature and a wish to find out where and when man was lost.

Secondly, while situating "I" among everything in nature, Zhuangzi presented the aesthetic pleasure of quietness and harmony resulted from the disinterestedness in utility and possession by creating four ideal personalities: the holy man, the sagas, the perfect man and the true man. The first one, "the holy man with all his integrity can merge everything under heaven into one" (8). He was described to have the most unbelievable figure who is "as amiable as a virgin, with his skin as white as ice and snow. He does not eat the grains, but sucks the wind, drink the dew, rides on the cloud, harnesses the flying dragon and roams beyond the four seas. By concentrating his spiritual power, he protects the creatures from the plague and ensures a bumper harvest." (*Zhuangzi*, 9) This imaginary figure pictured the supreme ideal image of living in nature. The pleasure lied in the inseparableness with the life of oneness. The ego of the holy man was in and through the life of oneness so that the natural being of "I" was endowed with an almighty capacity of existence at a harmonious interaction with natural things, the wind, the dew, the cloud and so on. The second one, the sagas, a key word which was most frequently appeared in the Book, "is not involved in worldly affairs. He does not take delight in seeking after or blindly clinging to Tao. He means something by saying nothing; he means nothing by saying something. By so doing he can be free from the physical body." (35)① "The sage keeps a peaceful mind not because peacefulness is good for him and thus he keeps a peaceful mind. It is because nothing in the world can disturb him that he keeps a peaceful mind." (201) When Zhuangzi talked about the sagas, he was referring to thepleasure of getting rid of the pursuing of fame and feat. The sagas maintained his position in the oneness of nature by withdrawing from any intended effort to be the dominator of the universe. This cooperates well with the Zhuangzi's belief that there was no manipulation and domination within the oneness of the universe. The aesthetic pleasure for the sagas was to achieve the inner quietness and peacefulness and to keep harmony with the environment. The individual happiness lied side by side with the harmony of every thing of oneness. Once one inclined to step out of the appropriate position within the oneness and ran after fame and feat, interest, possession and superiority either in spirit or material things, he

---

① In this paper "无谓有谓，有谓无谓，而游乎尘垢之外", I translate it into He means something by saying nothing; He means nothing by saying something. By so doing he can be free from the physical body."

would lose the pleasure of inner quietness and peace and suffer from the obsession of entangled disturbance of various desires and longings chained one by one, and which caused destruction to the holistic interaction with nature, and consequently drove human being to an alienated existential situation and to the ecological crisis we are addressing.

The third one, the perfect man, which was explained in the conversation between Confucius and Laozi, Confucius asked Laozi: "Would you tell me how your mind wanders in the great Tao?" (349) Laozi said, "He whose mind wanders in the great Tao has attained perfect beauty and perfect happiness. He who attains perfect beauty and wanders in perfect happiness is a perfect man" (349), Here Tao is closely associated with beauty and happiness. When Laozi went on explaining, we found that the beauty and happiness had been arrived at on the basis of respecting the diversified existence of lives. "Animals that feed on grass do not mind the change of swamps; water creatures do no mind the change of ponds. They can sustain minor changes when the basic living conditions remain the same. Joy, anger, grief and sorrow will not affect them in the least. The world is the place where all things co-exist." (349) Living one's own way without bothering the other existence demands a knowledge of the things in themselves. "The point is to learn from nature, to enter into its spirit, and to stop trying to impose upon it the arbitrary constraints which result from our belief in our own importance." (Bate, Green Studies Reader, 1)

The last one was the true man who is with the way: "He who comprehends purity and simplicity is called a "true man" (*Zhuangzi*, 251). The purity means being without foreign substance, being truly yourself; the simplicity means being without impairing the spirit, being cautious of protection of everything in its own way. "To know what the heaven can do and to know what man can do—that is the ultimate human knowledge." (89) Here the true man is supposed to know who he is and where he is in order to be in the oneness of the universe. The ethic is that to know oneself is for the sake of knowing the world and to know the world is for the sake of knowing oneself rather than for the sake of using and exploring it. The "I" and the world are interrelated existence instead of oppositional exploitation. The true man stressed on the interrelated and independent relationship between him and the natural beings, and on his position in the natural existence. He took the natural being as it was rather than as he thought it should be. To him simplicity and synchronic being with everything in nature is the truth for the way of human existence. In simplicity of human mind and consciousness, Zhaungzi was addressing the precondition of the unified position of human with the rest of the world. This revealed the ground on which the Zhaungzi's ethical conception was based.

The conception of the four ideal personalities appeared completely opposite to and even countered against that of the hero in modern tragedy tradition in which the hero was motivated by the success, by great achievement, by sacrifice to some belief, by the metaphysical morality, by fighting bravely and gloriously for a nation or a doctrine. According to Meeker, the conception of the hero constituted a strong force for historical progress and social development, and thus centralized the human world, the human society within the universe. The human society distinguished itself by assuming a dominating and manipulating role to the rest of the world. As is shown by many great tragedies, power prevailed in the cultural discourse through history. With the help of technology, the power ran desperately expanded against the natural world. In Joseph Meeker's *Comedy of Survival*, we read:

> Tragic literature is an appropriated source for information about the humanistic endorsement of ecological error, for tragedy is unusually inclusive of the values of civilization... Tragic literature is a mirror with impeccably sharp resolution and high selectivity... Tragic writers, like engineers have consistently chosen to affirm those values

which regard the world as mankind's exclusive property. (41)

It may be arbitrary to say that tragic heroic view of life has caused the ecological crisis; but it did help to build up the assumption of human superiority to the processes of nature which has justified human exploitation of nature without regard for the consequences to animals, plants, or the land (Meeker, 59). In literary ecology, there expressed a longing for the aesthetic pleasure of quietness and harmony. In other words, In order to end the long and disastrous warfare between mankind and the natural world, it may be necessary to cast a fundamental look towards the ethic way of treating the relationship between man and nature.

In Zhuangzi's ethic conception, the initiative concern of the relationship was with the world and then with the society. If we consider belief and the world view as a kind of input of the way to live and to live among other beings, the ethics would be the output of how the input would work. So ethic is for belief and belief is for ethic too. They are very much closely interrelated. The aesthetic works serves as the meter to measure as for how much the ethics is healthy. Since Zhuangzi grounded the belief in the life of oneness, his main ethical concern was about keeping the activity of completeness and put the diversity of lives in the first place as follows:

> Now I'd like to ask you a few questions. If a man sleeping in the damp is liable to get a back-ache or half-paralysis, will the same thing happen to an eel? If a man sitting in tree is liable to tremble with fear, will the same thing happen to an ape? Of the man, the eel and the ape, who knows their proper place to live in? Men eat meat; deer feed on grass; centipedes are fond of snake; owls like rats. Of the man, the deer, the centipede and the owl, who knows the right taste? An ape mates with a gibbon; a buck seeks after a doe; an eel plays with a fish. At the sight of Maoqiang and Xishi, beauties were admired by

men. (*Zhuangzi*, 33)

Diversity is the basic characteristic of ecosystem discovered by modern biology. We came to feel the ecological crisis when we realized how much the biodiversity had been destroyed. The concept of diversity sends out the ethic message of mutual respect among the species which indicates the awareness of presence of all. However as represented in literary history, the human beings alone were enlightened to the extent that their society was supposed to be the ultimate construction of the world and other beings existed only as the object of either the knowledge for human to see themselves or resources for the benefit of human being. Human history also turned out to be a history of increasingly indifferent and ignorant of the presence of other natural beings. In the process of ignoring the unified oneness that Zhuangzi's argued, human position was changing from certainty to uncertainty. It may sound arbitrary. But even pastoral poetry, which is considered as one of the representative genre of returning to nature and longing for the unified harmony with nature actually illustrates the fact that human beings wish to withdraw from taking themselves as a superior existence with regard to nature and the pastoral representation presented the movement of human tendency between the tension of the metaphysical speculation and the material reality, and it showed an fit-in effort to appreciate and enjoy the beauty of nature.

Fit-in

By fit-in, there implied a voluntary action whichmoves in from outside. There indicates a subject and object opposition of two parties, one of which remains stationary, and is supposed to be the object, while the other is finding a position in opposition to the object. By fit-in, the object is perceived as something meta-existence while the other party subjects itself to the drive of returning back to the objective existence.

This can beseen in the Chinese pastoral representation in Literature. After Warring period, in China, there have been two dominant representations of human ideal which can be best expressed by Mencius saying, to wit, you should dedicate yourself to the peace and order of the society when everything is favorable for your engagement. You may withdraw to a quiet place for self perfection when everything goes against you. In other words, one the one hand, it is Confucian ideal that one is obliged to devote oneself to the realization the perfect social order; on the other hand there always exists a strong drive from the inner heart to fit into the grand existence of nature world, that of Taoist ideal which mainly put oneness of man and nature relationship as the main concern. However they are by no means clearly separated, instead more or less commingled with each other most of the cases. The representation of Confusion idea, of the strict order of politics and family, assume the historical importance in the sense of exerting the humanity power. At the same time a call to tend to nature for self perfection and quietness composed a force countering the deterioration of the natural personality. That is what the pastoral poetry traditionalized by Tao Yuanming, followed by Libai, Sushi to name just a few, represented. Tao Yuanming (365? –427) lived during Jin dynasty which was a about seven hundred years away from Zhuangzi. Like most of the ancient Chinese intellectuals, he once was determined to contribute himself to the emperorgovernment. Disappointed with the corruptness of the relationship and sovereign, he quitted and went back home for a farmer's life and wrote more than 300 poems which influenced and started the pastoral tradition which continued up to the beginning of the 20th century in China.

Reading the poems by Tao Yuanming, one can see that there appeared a change in belief, aesthetic pleasure, and ethic construction from that of

Zhuangzi's, though he was acknowledged as the direct transmitter of Zhuangzi's natural view. He didn't represented nature as an autonomous oneness any longer, instead in his poetry, the nature was nothing more than a original place with the natural objects which could endow people the pleasure derived either from the beauty of the surrounding or from the simplicity of the relationships with regard to the complicated social relations. When the nature was narrowed down to a place, it would indicate a change of world view to look at the nature world from a holistic life body to a specific environment for human to live in. The attachment to a place could be understood from two levels, one is in the sense of possession which led to the accumulated economic drive of social development up to the industrialized and post industrialized today. The other is in the sense of memory which treated nature as a home or where man used to belong to, mostly the spiritual home. Here the later sense would be the one to be discussed, that is to say that the nature in pastoral representation was not believed as a live being, rather it is a place for the natural lovers to fit into.

In the first place, Tao's poems presented a belief in the perpetual time dimension of natural world, which means that the nature would be there forever though it was stationary, by contrast, human life was ephemeral. "The heaven lasts forever with the earth/While hills and rivers never change their worth. /The plants have always followed Nature's course, /With frost and dew as their empowering source. /Of all things, man is the paragon, but can not be compared with them. /He may be seen alive a while ago, / And will be dead and gone before you know. /" (Tao Yuanming, 79)① In the poem, the poet illustrated a puzzle fact that man was the paragon of all things, but where he should be among all the things? The positionless obsession troubled poet's mind. The positional thinking directly affected

① In this paper "谓人最灵智" I translate it as "Of all things, man is the paragon" to replace Wang's translation of "Of all things, man is listed on top".

people as for how to treat their life and things related to life. "Human life is rootless like a gale, /Floating like the dust along a trail. /It drifts and sails across the span of time," In Tao Yuanming's mind, human beings was no longer the original being. So when we were born on this world we should treat everything and everyone as brothers and sisters. Tao's pastoral poetry passed the message that people were supposed to cherish the life time and enjoy the beauty and pleasure of being with the wonderful nature. With nature as stationary as a place, man as a short timer, Tao Yuanming expressed a union through drinking wine, which played an important role in Chinese poet's lives. Even though there are no Dionysian God, in Chinese mythology, it did celebrate the ontological rejoice of human existence. "The things may live and die, rise and fall; /This everlasting law applies to all. /... summer and winter come and go, so is with human way. / Sagacious men who understands this truth/lead a hermit's life from early youth. Come on, hand a cup of wine to me/so that I will be in high glee day and night." (109) To the poet, the joy and happiness in drunken state beamed the truth of the life by losing oneself in the drink and forgetting about the possession of the material things but rather striving to reunite with everything.

When nature was taken as the place to be back to, the best way and ideal way to rejoin it is to enjoy the peaceful life in it "I pluck hedge-side chrysanthemums with pleasure/and see the tranquil southern mount in leisure. /The evening haze enshrouds it in fine weather/While flocks of birds are flying home together. /The view provides some veritable truth, / But my defining words seem to me uncouth." (113) In a way, the relationship of nature beings such as birds and mountains, flowers were used to be a mirror of human fit-in existence. Similar to Wordsworth's "Lines Written in Early Spring", Tao's thinking of the position of human being resorted to romantic imagination to feel the relevant relationship between the natural phenomena and the human life. Subjecting to natural being and persistence in being self preconditions the connection between the natural action and man's behavior. In Wordsworth's poem, we can't avoid the feeling that "his experience of natural phenomena, however, forces him to resist his education, his cultural training, just as his poem challenges our learned cultural presupposition that human consciousness alienates us from physical nature". (Kroeber, 45) Similarly in Tao's poems, we see a picture which The aesthetic pleasure and the personality Tao maintained in his poetic expression supported by a realistic country life he practiced. In his life, he proclaimed a strong sense of satisfaction in sharp contrast to the escalating desire and longing of the urban life.

> I've loathed the secular world since I was a boy/While hills and mountains have filled me withjoy. /By mistake I sought mundane careers/And got entrapped in them for thirty years. /Birds in cage would long for wooded hills; /Fish in the pond would yearn for flowing rills. /So I Reclaim the land in southern fields. /To suit my bent for reaping farmland yields. /My farm contains a dozen mu of ground; /My cottage has eight or nine rooms around. /The elm and willow screen the backside eaves/While peach and plum tress shade my yard with leaves/The distant village dimly looms somewhere, /With smoke from chimneys drifting in the air. /In silent country lanes a stray dog barks; /Amid the mulberry tress cocks crow with larks. /My house escapes form worldly moil or gloom/While ease and quiet permeates my private room. /When I escape from the besiege state, /I live a free and easy life again (Tao Yuanming, 53)①

① In this paper, I used *secular world* to replace *madding crow*, madding crowd means more of people's relation, while secular world implies more of the pursuing of political fame and material possession. I don't think Tao Yuanming was tired of the human relations but rather he was tired of the political affairs and the corrupted political regime. Second the last line but one I used *besieged society* to replace *the bitter strife with man* forthe same reason.

In the poem two places were mentioned, one is the natural world with mountains, pond, fields, trees and forest, dogs and birds, villages and houses. The combination of the images showed that a simple life would fit into the natural phenomena, and enabled people a simple and clear and pleasant mind as also proclaimed by Henry David Thoreau; the other world is the secular one, or to be specifically the political life which was compared to the besieged state, the cage, where the freedom was deprived, thus where the natural personalities were threatened to be polluted away. The natural world was considered to be an original world where the people were supposed to be from and where people missed and made an effort to fit-in again. The realistic description of the country surrounding deliberately built up a mood for a free existence of which was missed for so long. That strengthened the charms of the simple life and the pleasure derived from country life.

The aesthetic pleasure derived from the simple life owned much to the feeling of being satisfied with a simple life on one's own farm as practiced by Thoreau as well; "*My farm contains a dozen mu of ground; /My cottage has eight or nine rooms around.*" Here the pleasure was closely connected with satisfaction, the opposite of urban insatiable consumption, and which can result in a very mutual respective and interdependent relationship with nature. As we know, Tao Yuanming lived a very poor life and sometimes he couldn't even afford a from-hand-to-mouth life. But the suffering from the material shortage didn't mean much when he was devoted to the thinking of the appropriate position of human being in this world. The devotion expressed a supportive power which could help the poet maintain his free self not to be driven away by the intertwined secular material desire. The force arose from the memory of harmonious union with nature, which opposed to the hierarchical social position, and which supported the poet's belief in his satisfaction with simple life. This memory persisted and enabled the poet to immerse himself in the pleasure of finding his place in the surrounding rather than in the exploitative hierarchical society. Buell said when talking about the aesthetics of relinquishment: "the effect of environment consciousness on the perceiving self, as I see it, is not primarily to fulfill it, to negate it, or even to complicate it, although all of these may seem to happen. Rather the effect is most fundamentally to raise the question of the validity of the self as the primary focalizing device for both writer and reader. To make one wonder for instance whether the self is as interesting an object of study as we supposed whether the world would become more interesting if we could see it from the perspective of a wolf, a sparrow, a river, a stone." (Buell, 179). To some extent, Tao's poems provided us with such implication of relinquishment by seeing the world as the original ground for the self to fit into, at least with an effort to connect oneself with the nature being rather than detach oneself from it.

Buell's aesthetic relinquishment was built up on the analysis of Thoreau's tradition. In the first half of 19th century, with the fast tempo of industrialization and urbanization marching into the nature, David Thoreau also advocated such a call, "simplicity, simplicity, simplicity". The paradoxical fact is that they were 1500 years apart from each other. This may confuse our conception of progress in history, but pushes us to touch the standpoint of the ethic proclamation of simplicity. When Tao Yuanming praised simplicity, he was considering nature metaphorically as a home to be back to. He believed that that was the place which could provide him with ease and freedom. He attached his self to the place. The attachment to nature arose from the opposition to the tiredness of social detachment of relationship. He celebrated the joy in drinking which to him could draw him closer to natural being. This manifested the fit-in tendency with regard to nature. However, Thoreau's simplicity suggested a strong anxiety and worry, which associated with place destruction common to the present environmental writings, and which resulted from the progress of industrialization and the hegemony of the political power. There is no need to list the consequences upon nature caused by the impetuous progress. Different from the Tao Yuanming's fit-in pastoral poetry, the representation of the contemporary environmental literature which shared Thoreau's worry and anxiety revealed the Diaspora state of human beings.

Diaspora

The Dictionary meaning of Diaspora refers to the dispersion of the Jews after their exile. Among the rich cultural, historical and economic implications of diaspora, detachment from home is the symbolic image reflecting the ecological human position in the context of industrialization and urbanization.

China embarked on the boat of new civilization, the western modernization or industrialization, at the turn of twentieth century, waving goodbye to the long and old feudalist society. Even though, there was no such an act as enclosure movement happened in England, as is described by Raymond Williams: "yet, there is a sense in which the idea of the enclosures, localized to just that period in which the Industrial Revolution was beginning, can shift our attention from the real history and become an element of that very powerful myth of modern England in which the transition from a rural to an industrial society is seen as a fall, the true cause and origin of our social suffering and disorder." (Williams, 96), the modernization movement at the turn of the 20th century which meant to rouse Chinese people's national responsibility did change Chinese people's conception of place and idea of human position on earth. Chinese people who used to root their lives in the order of nature and that of Confusion came to the awareness of believing in science and technology and the change of human welfare and dignity in the name of democracy and in the awakening of individuality. In a century, particularly at the second half of

20th century, the revolution and reformation against the tradition, family and dictatorial order achieved unprecedented progress in the sphere of economy, consumption and social structure through accelerated industrialization and urbanization.

Of course, there is no denying that the industrialization and urbanization brought a new dimension to people both in material lives and technological imagination. Materially, the determinism of natural order has been gradually replaced by the dependence on the human technological power, in other words, the change of economic structure has something to do with the shift of belief in human power. Unfortunately the change of economic structure most severely affects the natural environment especially in the western part of China, whence is most of the contemporary environmental writing in China. Chinese environmental writing for example, Jiangrong's *Wolf Totem* (2004) and Guo Xuebo's *Desert Wolf* (2006) and *Silver Fox* (2006) tended to locate the background in the changing economic structure of Inner Mongolia, and spotlighted the critical loss of top soil and groundwater, deforestation and desertification. Technological imagination take nature mainly as material resources which could be attained by exploration and exploitation for the benefit of human beings, rather than with the permanent existence in opposition to human being's fleeting lives. With the exploration and exploitation into the nature, people who have been facilitated by the development of science and technology have not been able to satisfy with their basic material needs but rather run after their escalated material desire and arrived at the augmentation of population which has turned out to be the ironical manifestation of human power (Karl Kroeber, 1994).

Spiritually, the reliance on the unified power of human, heaven and earth was gradually replaced by the slogan that man could conquer all including heaven and earth, which were represented to the extreme in Chinese literature during the middle of 20th century. In other words, the anthropocentric thinking established its place in people's mind and allowed human beings to assume the dominant role. However the domination had to struggle against the destruction, Just as Rechael Carson put it: "The "control of nature" is a phrase conceived in arrogance, born of the Neanderthal age of biology and philosophy, when it was supposed that nature exists for the convenience of man. The concepts and practices of applied entomology for the most part date from that Stone Age of science. It is our alarming misfortune that so primitive a science has armed itself with the most modern and terrible weapons, and that in turning them against the insects it has also turned them against the earth." (Carson, 297) Consequently through the writing there foretold a self exiling story and home of earth became a relative word to refer to a place to stay in. Diaspora came to be the theme of human position.

This paper doesn't mean to stand against the development of human beings, but rather to investigate human position with regard to nature by literature, and look up at the question: where are we going?

Such question emerged from the reporting documentary writing with which Chinese environmental literature started in the middle of the 1980s and gradually joined by other genres like allegorical fiction represented by Guo Xuebo, Zhefu. In the reporting documentary writing, we have been confronted with the shocking facts of deforestation, water exhaustion, desert expansion, and the endangered species. Like the prefix de-suggested, the representation of human position in the contemporary literature implied the tendency of leaving, or dispersing homelessly. Xugang who is considered the first writer to address the ecological problems in literary creation in China exposed the situation of woodcutting, the related desert expansion and water exhaustion from south to north and from east to west in China. He warned people earnestly of their action in his *Wake up, woodcutter* by saying "Our ancestor's grave is in the forest, our children's lives lies in the hand of the forest. Please put down your axe, Human being, we need to regret." (The Fallen Land 65) In the warning, there expressed a strong anxiety and worry of Diaspora. According to Xugang, when people are regardless of the other beings, such as the trees and overcut them, and when they are careless about the interrelated relationship with grassland, animals and overexploit the environment, they are actually driving themselves away from the place where they are living. Not to mention the clean air, the necessary rain, which are essential to people's lives, the greentrees, plants constitutes undeniably home of people.

The power of the documentary reports lies in joining the facts with the force of imagination and worked on the emotion of both writers and readers. In one of the facts he described in his reporting, the example of Shazhuyu county in Qinghai province, we read that because of the change of the economic activity, people cut down the tress and swept off the grassland. As a result, the desert expansion have been accelerated and thus caused the self dispersion.

> The desert expansion almost swallowed up the county and made it disappear from the map of Qinghai province. A county which had been a rich one with beautiful water and grassland and self contained Shepard lives until the 1940s was replaced quickly by a yellow heap of sand. The Local residence lost hope and move out and left their homeland with tears. (Xugang, 110, trans. mine)

The reporting realistically depicted the reality of local Diaspora which people were actually driving themselves out of their own homeland. It is by no means an isolated effect. It tells something of the slow moving consequences caused jointly by broken belief and absence of ethical care of a broader dimension, since the belief in nature and care of nature were marginalized by the sweeping effect of the anthropocentric material development. The associated reality of would-be Diaspora speak out an urgent message of the rethinking, reconsidering of man and nature relationship and man's position in this world. It is not a question of whether man should care about nature and plant trees, as people from Shazhuyu county did, but rather it is a matter of whether there are spaces left for people to disperse, and whether there is time for people to repent? With the deterioration of desert expansion, "people have started and speeded up their escape continually. But the most tragic question is we can escape to nowhere" (*The Fallen Land*, 112, trans, mine).

As far as the ecological human position is concerned, Diaspora metaphorically unrolled the fate as well the choice of mankind. Earth is our home, but obviously the environmental situation is saying that we are driving ourselves away from earth. We are making earth more a place not suitable for us to live in as demonstrated in most of literary reports which are unrolling the picture of leaving home tendency by showing us the facts of water exhaustion, deforestation, desert expansion. The literary reporter's passion of arousing people's awareness of tragic and pessimistic environmental future may sometimes not be in coincide with or even counter against the grand view of fast development of the big cities. But if we look up and stare into the forest of buildings in the cities, this is really no longer the diversified home of earth with various living communities of various species and sceneries.

While literary reporters put up the realist picture of Diaspora by telling people the endangered home resulted from the deforestation, desert expansion, water exhaustion, the ecological fiction writers like Guo Xuebo and Zhefu, have illustrated a metaphorical picture of the spiritual Diaspora and push the choice in front of us too. Guo Xuebo, a writer from Innermogolia, tended to show us in his desert novels the sharp contrast between the fallen humanity of man and the natural beauty of the endangered animals. In his novel we read that, it was hard for mankind to resist the alienation of humanity as they became more and more greedy and ill natured. They tended to become so easily lunatic, aggressive, indifferent, and hostile; however the animals were represented as a creature with the caring natural instinct which outmatched that of humanity. They were depicted under Guo Xuebo's pen as so caring and supportive and kind in the treatment of relationship that the characters chose to stay with them rather than go back to the human society. In the ending of both novels, *The Wolf Kid* and *The Silver Fox*, he told the story symbolically that Xiaolong in *The Wolf Kid* and Shanmei in *The Silver Fox* would rather go to the wild with the wolf or the fox than go back home and back to the human society. Of course it had to be understood symbolically. On the one hand, it could be understood as both leaving and returning. By leaving, it referred to an act of self exile from home and went into homeless state which echoed the literary reporting of moving away form home because of the natural disaster directly inflicted by human behavior like woodcutting and water pollution. But here the self exile associated with spiritual illness and alienation. By returning, it implies the symbolic meaning of going back to nature again, and of rediscovering human position with other life species in order to recover the peaceful state of mind. Shanmei was afflicted with strange lunatic spirit, which also struck all the women in the village. While she was not in the clear mind, she was raped by Hu Dalun, the village leader and later saved by the endangered fox and started her interdependent life with the fox. When Shanmei's father-in-law, who used to try to hunt the fox, and now came to the desert to look for his daughter-in-law, saw the mutual care between Shanmei and the Fox, he felt great relief and gave up hunting. After Shanmei came back to her normal senses, she chose to stay with the fox. The novel ended shockingly with that Shanmei, her father-in-law, and the narrator decided to stay with the fox in the desert instead of going back to the village. The message that the author wanted to pass was very obvious.

Human mind is in serious illness which is leading human to the

> self destruction. The only way out, the only hope to survive is to return to nature. It is only by going back to nature can human being restore to his normal state. This is the prophecy of the silver fox. This is the inspiration from totem of the desert. (*The Silvery Fox*, 301, trans. mine)

One the other hand, however, the symbolic ending is very likely to indicate another very sarcastic meaning: that we are maltreating nature ends up mistreating ourselves, that we are conquering all ends up losing our own home. Instead of unrealistically returning back to nature which was very ambiguous and unknown, human beings have to take the fate of leaving home. While human being killed off the other species, used up the resources, he was bringing himself to an end with the endangered nature. That is the "prophecy" of the novel. Ecological writing is assuming a very eager role to speak out the prophecy. The writers bear on the responsibility to sound it out even if the voice is very simple.

Conclusion

Ecocritical survey of human position in Chinese literature is a tentative effort to figure out how much the thinking of position of humanity could be represented in the literary representation. From Zhuangzi's unification to the present environmental Diaspora scene, we find that the thinking of human position changes over history and is particularly associated with the aesthetic belief. The idea of unification rooted its belief in that the world is a unified life, and man was a synchronic life form and the great pleasure lied in maintaining the independent self on the condition of not intruding into other beings. Yet, the representation of fit-in tendency as is shown in the pastoral poetry took the world as a permanent metaexistence in contrast to the ephemeral sojourn of human being. Sensual experience of natural beauty was closely connected with the feeling of belonging and the self was subject to a certain moral power. Great moral importance was attached to the satisfaction with simplicity. However the Diaspora picture is painted with the brush of anthropocentric thinking facilitated with the fast development of science and technology. The physical world in modern belief is perceived to be subject to human being's manipulation and manufacture. The human self is called to bear on the task of revelation. So, the gloomy representation of the Diaspora scene posed a challenge to anthropocentric belief. It is human beings who are creating almighty wanders and yet at the same time destroying his own standing place, his home. Thus, we have enough room to cast an optimistic trust on anthropocentric belief while pointing fingers to it. Never before in history have human beings considered their individual being as the reality to believe in as much as in modern age and never before in history have human beings realized that their reality would be endangered if it was independent of the reality of the ecological integrity. For the first time in the history of humanity we stand face to face with a choice imposed up us to response to the refrain of the question: "Where we lived, and what we lived for."

Works Cited:

1. Anderson, Lorraine, eds. *Sisters of the Earth: Women's prose and Poetry About Nature.* New York: Random, 1991.
2. Branch, Michael P. and Slovic, Scott, eds. *The ISLE Reader: Ecocriticism, 1993 – 2003.* Athen: University of Georgia Press, 2003.
3. Buell, Lawrence. *The Environmental Imagination: Thoreau, Nature Writing, and the Formation of American Culture.* Cambridge: Harvard University Press, 1995.
4. Carson, Rachael. *The silent Spring.* Boston: Houghton, 1994.
5. Coupe, Laurence, eds. *Green Studies Reader: From Romanticism to Ecocriticism.* London: Routledge, 2000.
6. Glotfelty, Cheryll & Fromm, Harold, eds. *The Ecocriticism Reader: Landmarks in*

Literary Ecology. Athens: University of Georgia Press, 1996.

7. Guo Xuebo. *The Silvery Fox*. Guilin: Lijiang Press, 2006.
8. Kroeber, Karl. *Ecological Literary Criticism: Romantic Imagining and the Biology of Mind*. New York: Columbia University Press, 1994.
9. Meeker, Joseph W. *The Comedy of Survival: Studies in Literary Ecology*. New York: Charles Schibner's Sons., 1972.
10. Reich Charles. *The Greening of America*. New York: Random House, 1970.
11. Wang Rongpei, Trans. *The Complete Works of Tao Yuanming*. Changsha: Hunan People's Press, 2003. (Library of Chinese Classic.)
12. Wang Rongpei, Trans. *Zhuangzi*. Changsha: Hunan People's Press, 1999. (Library of Chinese Classic.)
13. Williams, Raymond. *The Country and the City*. New York: Oxford University Press, 1973.
14. Xu Gang. *The Fallen Land*. Beijing: People's Literature Press, 2005.

From Shanghai Beauty to Earth Mother: The Retreat of Sexuality and the Rise of Productivity in Wang Anyi's Writings

CHEN Dandan*

中文摘要 本文通过细读文本，探讨王安忆小说中的空间与女性形象的变迁。论文聚焦于王安忆如何在作品中创建出一种诗意空间：劳动作为女性乌托邦。通过展现身体、性别与空间之间的多层互动，以及男性特质与女性特质之间的复杂关系，王安忆在不同的作品中追踪女性身体与意识的生长，女性意识如何作为一种“无意识的意识”萌生与变化。在很多上海故事中，上海被呈现为娱乐与消费之地，但王安忆的写作逐渐将这座城市从娱乐与消费的领域推入生产领域，并在此领域中构建自己的女性乌托邦。王安忆对上海的勾勒不是线性时间层面上的叙述，而是通过对不同空间的描画，展现这座城市的时间维度。如此，在她笔下，上海的空间将时间与人们在时间层面上的各种意识与感知也通统结晶化。本文将主要探讨三部作品：

* 陈丹丹，哈佛大学文学博士，现任美国纽约州立大学法明代尔州立学院历史、政治与地理系/科学、技术与社会系助理教授，兼任哈佛大学费正清中国研究中心研究员，主要研究海外新儒家与中国思想史、现当代中国文学与文化。

《逃之夭夭》《富萍》《天香》。通过强调“劳动”与“生产性”，王安忆将关于女性身体的话语，转向关于“生产”与“劳作”的话语。在生产与劳动中发展出的女性友谊与互助，也就此比男女之间的关系更为重要。劳动中“女人性”作为核心与“男人性”的缺席，使得“生产”与“劳作”的空间也就此呈现为女性主义与女性乌托邦的空间。

关键词 王安忆；空间；身体；性别；女性乌托邦

Abstract This essay explores the writing of space, body, and sexuality in contemporary China through a close analysis of the stories of Wang Anyi, one of the most important female writers in contemporary China. I argue that Wang's work not only addresses these themes, but also presents the complexities of China as it transitions from a pre-socialist to a socialist society and onward toward a socialist market economy. I especially focus on Wang's construction of a poetic space—labor as feminine utopia—in her stories. While examining the relationships among body, sexuality, and space, as well as the dialectics between femininity and masculinity, Wang traces the maturing of female bodies and the development of feminine consciousness as unconscious consciousness. In many writings on Shanghai, urban scene is primarily described as one where people pursue entertainment. But Wang's writings gradually turn the city from a realm of entertainments into one of production, from which she constructs her feminine utopia. Instead of providing a linear narrative of Shanghai history, Wang's writings capture the city's temporal dimensions by spatially remapping it. The urban space of Shanghai crystallizes time and people's temporal sensibilities in contemporary China. In my consideration of three of her works: *Peach Trees in Full Blossom* (*Tao zhi yaoyao*), *Fu Ping*, and

Scent of Heaven (*Tianxiang*), I focus on interactions among body, sexuality, and the production of feminine space. By emphasizing labor and productivity, Wang turns discourses around female bodies into discourses about production. Once sexuality is framed in terms of production, female friendship and mutual support eclipse relations between men and women. With an emphasis on womanliness and the absence of manliness, the space of production becomes one of femininity.
Keywords Wang Anyi; Space; Body; Sexuality; Feminine Utopia

In much literature centered on Shanghai, urban space is described primarily as a space of entertainment. But Wang Anyi's writings gradually turn that space into one of production, from which she constructs a feminine utopia. There was also a historical side to the development of femininity in her stories. In her *Love in a Small Town* (*Xiaocheng zhi lian*, 1986), for instance, Wang's discovery of the body grows from discourses on individualism or individual liberation, which belong to the pioneering literary and intellectual discourse of the 1980s. In later Shanghai narratives, Wang's treatment of the body is incorporated into a set of more complicated discourses that become intertwined in the context of contemporary China. These trends, forces, and discourses include labor, femininity, production, space, and society's commercialization, and are rooted in specific political/cultural situations of China in its various historical periods. In this sense, Wang's writings represent an important window through which we can deeply examine the social transformations and the spiritual characteristics of contemporary China. As for her presentation of women, the transition from the image of the Shanghai beauty to that of earthmother shows Wang's reflection on the socialist experience, which echoes the shift of socialist China towards a market society as well as

Wang's own reflections on this transformation. By joining the image of earth mother to labor as utopia, Wang brings new emphasis to the legacies of socialist China that can function as sources of resistance against the processes of commercialization and alienation across society.

Various approaches to Wang's urban writings have appeared in print, but few scholars have deeply examined the development of her treatment of the body, sexuality, and urban space, or the complicated relationships among these that have taken shape in the course of China's dramatic transformation in its contemporary periods. While understanding Wang as a representative writer of the materiality of Shanghai, the scholarship has focused more on the external landscapes of Shanghai (the form or material world of the city) in Wang's writings and largely neglected the city's internal logic. The details of everyday life depicted in Wang's writings are much discussed, but the deeper social foundations of those details and the metaphysical or transcending level above everyday life Wang pursues have been overlooked. Some scholars have focused on Wang's writings about myth and memory. For example, Howard Y. F. Choy links Wang's writing on Shanghai with her work on Singapore and calls attention to the parallel of prose writing about urban space and its poetic prehistory; however, Choy does not explore how Wang's presentation of spaces is rooted in her refreshed reflections on history and social change. [①] In addition, the presentation of labor, production, and productivity in Wang's writings and how Wang includes these three issues in her treatment of body, sexuality, and space have not been given their due. This paper takes a close look at the interaction among these elements in Wang's literary remapping of China's constantly changing temporal-spatial structure in its transformation from a

---

① Howard Y. F. Choy, "From Pacific Ocean to Gobi Desert: Wang Anyi's Migratory Mythology," in Choy, *Remapping the Past: Fictions of History in Deng's China, 1979 - 1997*, Leiden: Brill, 2008, pp. 67 - 79.

pre-modern, pre-socialist country to a modern, socialist one.

Before I start my arguments in each section, I would like to provide some explanations of two key concepts: labor and production. In this paper, I would like to use them in terms of Marxist definitions and their Sinicized forms (*laodong* and *shengchan*) in the context of modern China. My focus will be the representation of labor (*laodong*) and production (*shengchan*) and the space of labor and production in Wang Anyi's writings, and how this kind of representation adds another dimension to the tempo-spatial structure of Shanghai. Wang not only describes places of labor, but also depicts places of production. Here, production not only refers to production of physical goods or materials, but also includes productions of thoughts at the spiritual level. In *Age of Enlightenment* (*Qimeng shidai*, 2007), Wang highlights this kind of space of production where people exchanged their ideas and produced new understandings. Since the story of *Fu Ping* (2001) was set in the Socialist period without relations of exploitation, labor is not commercialized labor; Wang's passion for that era also prevented her from depicting labor as politicized labor; Her writings about labor are more like pure worship of labor as something that can turn wandering human beings into subjects of production and masters of their own bodies. Labor, in this sense, becomes something that can produce one's dignity and identity.

In his "Narratives on Labor or the Utopia of Labor," Cai Xiang traces the genealogy of the concept of labor (laodong) in the intellectual and literary history of twentieth-century China. After emphasizing the concept of "laboring man" (laodong de ren), Cai argues that,

> From any perspective, Marx remains the most profound thinker on the questions of labor. Not only does Marx's deep analysis of labor and the production process explore the intimate relation between capital and surplus value, but at the same time his labor theory of value

proposes that the proletariat alone is the subject of history. ①

In Wang Anyi's writings, we can also see a consistent search for the "subjects of history," which is crystallized in her depiction of laboring men or women. Here I also want to argue that the term "laodong" (labor) in Chinese is a Sinicized Marxist term. It not only consists the meaning of labor as Marx used it originally, but also includes a dimension of "shengchan" (production). Thus, the term "laodong zhe" (laborers, or laboring men or women) has more implications of subjectivity in the Chinese context. In Wang's fictional world, there is a combination of space of production (as she describes in *Scent of Heaven*) and space of labor (as she describes in *Fu Ping*). However, the laboring men or women in *Fu Ping* also gained their subjectivity not because what they produced, but because they were laboring.

From Shanghai Beauty to Earth Mother (*Dimu*): The Retreat of Sexuality and the Rise of Productivity

From the 1980s to the 2000s, Wang's writings have retreated from issues of sexuality and increasingly embraced productivity. She has integrated both sexuality and productivity into her representations of cities. In "Passion and Love in Hong Kong" (*Xianggang de qingyu ai*, 1993) Hong Kong is represented by the two women protagonists. In *The Song of Everlasting Sorrow* (*Changhe ge*, 1995), Shanghai finds its beauty in the image of Wang Qiyao, who takes third place in the Miss Shanghai Competition. Throughout the novel, Wang Qiyao's beauty has a power that

① Cai, Xiang, *Revolution and Its Narratives: China's Socialist Literary and Cultural Imaginaries, 1949 – 1966*, edited and translated by Rebecca E. Karl and Xueping Zhong, Durham and London: Duke University Press, 2016, p. 254.

not only changes her fate, but also brings her wealth and men's adoration. Although she chose to work as a nurse based at home after her lover Mr. Li dies, her daily work is never emphasized. Wang Qiyao is a symbol of sexuality, and this eventually causes her death. The issue of productivity is at best obscured in this story. Similarly, in *I Love Bill* (*Wo ai bi'er*, 1995), the heroine A San gradually losses her productivity as a painter when she becomes a prostitute, essentially turning herself into a commodity. However, starting from *Fu Ping* (2001), Wang Anyi gradually changed her approaches to sexuality and productivity. She began to represent the two as intertwined and opposite. Instead of highlighting sexuality, Wang often describes the improvement of a character's productivity by describing the retreat of sexuality. For example, the spiritual growth of the heroine Yu Xiaoqiu in *Peach Trees in Full Blossom* is represented as the disappearance of her feminine beauty and her sexual attractiveness. In *Fu Ping*, the lead character is not at all sexually attractive, but she is a figure through which Wang Anyi discovers the power of labor and productivity.

As Wang turns her focus to women as subjects who discover their subjectivities in labor (*laodong*) and production (*shengchan*), the city of Shanghai becomes a space of production that obtains its own self-identity. By this transition from object of fetishism to subject of labor, Wang recalls an older image of the city, not as a place for consumerism, but a poetic space for labor. She discovers the poetics of labor in this space of production. Moreover, Wang's discovery of the space of production is not only linked to her discovery of the margins of the city, but also integrated with the transformation of images of the body in her writings.

The body possesses external features and internal energies in Wang's stories. At the earlier stage of her writings, Wang highlights the former. The works I mentioned above, "Passion and Love in Hong Kong", *The Song of Everlasting Sorrow*, and *I Love Bill* are all good examples. As she develops her characters' external features, Wang differentiates among various types of sexuality and femininity. In *The Song of Everlasting Sorrow*, Wang Qiyao's beauty is characterized as graceful and fashionable, and is identified with the modern face of the city, even though she came from a normal family instead of a wealthy one. In contrast, Jiang Lili, the daughter of a rich family, becomes a female cadre in a new Socialist regime, where her feminine features are obscured by her role, by her attire. This contrast of "modern, sexually attractive" versus socialist seems more a stereotype than an effective device. While Wang has insisted that her primary purpose in writing *The Song of Everlasting Sorrow* was to criticize the "Shanghai modern," the work in fact seems to worship it. Because her effort to discuss socialist Shanghai was neglected by the novel's readers and critics, Wang has tried to make her critique of the modern more explicit in her later writings. Thus, in *Peach Trees in Full Blossom*, the stereotyped description of socialist cadres as less than feminine disappears. Wang wants to look into the complicated nature of femininity and sexuality when they encounter revolution and Socialist reconstruction.

In *Peach Trees in Full Blossom*, the beauty of the heroine Yu Xiaoqiu is considered vulgar (*su*), which causes Yu to feel ashamed. Similarly, her mother is also considered vulgar. [①]But Yu's father is portrayed as very sexually attractive, even having certain feminine features. Wang uses many adjectives that include the keyword "clear" (*qing*) to describe him. [②]She presents Yu's father initially by setting him against certain backgrounds. We first see the figure of the young man gazing from a window where he has lifted a corner of the plain curtain, which creates a clear framing of the

---

① Wang Anyi, *Peach Trees with Full Blossom* (Tao zhi yaoyao), Kunming: Yunnan People's Press, 2009, p. 17.

② Ibid., p. 16.

appearance of this important character. ①Wang continues to highlight the interplay between the image of this character and the background against which he appears. The first time Yu's mother sees him, he is shy and hides himself immediately once he realizes that she is looking at him. In Wang's description, he is like a lady who keeps herself in her inner chamber. The second time Yu's mother sees him, he is playing a girl's game with his little sister. Wang's description this time runs:

> This young man in a blue cloth tunic whitened from being washed so many times looked like a beautiful girl hiding there in the shadow of the pear tree's flowers. ②

The third time Yu's mother sees him, she is impressed by his good looks: "His skin is so clear that it is almost transparent, because of his plain and simple life." ③

As Wang Anyi describes him, this man looks like a virgin. ④He is too weak to be able to produce anything or contribute productively. Clearly, Wang uses this character to highlight the strengths of Yu Xiaoqiu and her mother. Her feminization of a male character recognizes and highlights the internal energy of women, which she puts forward in the vulgar, buoyant, and sexually exuberant images of Yu Xiaoqiu and her mother. Yu matured earlyand grew up fast. ⑤She is described as ripe and desirable. Wang takes a long paragraph to describe her rich and complex beauty: there is light coming from inside. There is internal growth, like a plant that goes from

---

① Wang Anyi, *Peach Trees with Full Blossom* (Tao zhi yaoyao), Kunming: Yunnan People's Press, 2009, p. 16.

② Ibid.

③ Ibid.

④ Ibid.

⑤ Ibid., p. 66.

sprout to full flower. This plant metaphor pertains also to the growth of internal space, subjective space.

By focusing on Yu's body as it grows through various stages, Wang Anyi constructs the distinction between inner and exterior space. The former is related to individual consciousness; the latter is rooted in the political and social situation in China at that time. With the growth of her body, Yu experiences the conflict between an individual body as a kind of natural force and the social body as a crystallization of its social and cultural world. Her beauty, being too sexually exuberant,① is not deemed suitable for revolutionary dance and song. ②The retreat of her sexual attractiveness was pushed into its extreme by the end of the story, when Yu is described as looking like a woman from the countryside. In this sense, Wang has transcended the stereotyped representation of Shanghai women as fashionable beauties. Here Wang has taken up a tradition from Eileen Chang: creating images of the earth mother.

In her essay "Speaking of Women" (*Tan nuren*), Eileen Chang expresses appreciation of the image of an earth mother described in Eugene O'Neill's *The Great God Brown*: a strong, quiet, sexually attractive woman, a prostitute with big breasts and ample hips. She does everything slowly but well. She is as lazy as a beast. This woman is like a holy cow that forgets time but has its own eternal goal. She loves all people and cherishes the dead. She is linked to the productivity of the earth and the eternal return of the four seasons. ③ In Eileen Chang's writings, the earth mother refers to a type of woman who possesses a strong character and can survive any situation, especially in times of chaos or crisis. Wang Jiaorui, one of the

---

① Wang Anyi, *Peach Trees with Full Blossom* (Tao zhi yaoyao), Kunming: Yunnan People's Press, 2009, p. 70.

② Ibid., pp. 82, 89.

③ Eileen Chang, "Speaking of Women," in *Written on Water*, New York: Columbia University Press, 2005, pp. 81 – 91.

heroines in *Red Rose*, *White Rose*, can be viewed as an earth mother, because she is determined, faithful to love, and bravely keeps her dignity even when her lover turns out to be a coward. Yan Geling is another writer who has made good use of the earth mother image in characters like Wang Putao in the novel *The Ninth Widow*. This type of woman not only has a kind of sexual beauty, but is able to survive as producer and laborer ("*shengchan zhe*" and "*laodong zhe*"), and hence is capable of rescuing men, nation, and history.

In Wang Anyi's writings, the transition from Shanghai beauty to earth mother is evident in both the external features and internal nature of her female characters. The image of Fu Ping in Wang's novel *Fu Ping* marks an important turning point in this transition. Fu Ping is not sexually attractive at all. Wang especially emphasizes that her face is a bit dull. Thus, this image also marks the retreat of sexuality from Wang's treatment of women. But does Wang depict her as an earth mother? At the first glance, she does not seem to display the external features of an earth mother. However, she always looks at people directly when she talks to them; this was not customary in urban China and gives her a bit of an edge. When she first arrives in Shanghai from the countryside, she has red cheeks and coarse, weathered skin; after she has lived in Shanghai a while, the red cheeks, considered a sign of rural life, disappear; this makes her seem a bit more shrewd. One important trait does bring her close to the image of the earth mother: her sturdy body. In addition to her thick wrists, the back of her neck and back are muscular. Thus, she can lift a 55 – pound bag of rice. ①

Even so, Wang emphasizes that she possesses a kind of feminine charm, which comes not only from her rural freshness, but also from her youth and gender. Here, we glimpse a hidden discourse on sexuality, although it is still eclipsed by Fu Ping's capacity to produce. At the novel's

---

① Wang Anyi, *Fu Ping*, Taipei: Maitian Press, 2001, pp. 31 – 32.

end, Wang implies that Fu Ping is pregnant, which gives her another key feature associated with the earth mother, fecundity.

Compared to Fu Ping, the heroine Yu Xiaoqiu in Wang's novel *Peach Trees in Full Blossom* has many obvious aspects associated with an earth mother, such as big breasts and other "erotic features". The "vulgar" body of Yu expresses an earth mother character, her strength and toughness. Initially these external features are in conflict with the character's internal qualities, however, by the end of this story, Yu has reached harmony and balance between body and mind:

> The healthy and ample shape of her figure has become strong after giving birth to a baby at this age. She looks like a peasant woman who has grown up doing manual labor in natural and outdoor environments and in unrefined love. In her body you'd never see the "cat eyes" associated with a "Xishi of the factory".① It all came about from a vigorous life force that radiated from her to take vivid shape in her physical being. Now that quality dives to a deeper place inside her. It is like flowers turning into fruit after being in full blossom. The splendid external (of the body) becomes quiet and plain, as her vitality is filling, filling, filling the internal, to flow out and encircle her surroundings in another unseen mode.②

Yu Xiaoqiu's features match those of the earth mother Eugene O'Neill describes in *The Great God Brown.* As a mother, she produces new life. The emphasis on her looking like a peasant woman strengthens her rootedness in the earth. Never a coward, she always takes responsibility for things she has done or should do.

---

① Xishi, was one of the four famous beauties of ancient China.

② *Peach Trees with Full Blossom*, p. 170.

The Conflation of the Spaces of Production and Sexuality

The interplay between sexuality and productivity takes place in space in Wang's work. Wang uses space at three levels: not only the material but also the gendered and class-associated. She turns the city landscape of Shanghai into various miniatures by something like sociological analysis. As Howard Y. F. Choy has noted, Wang's families of "comrades" keep drifting around Shanghai's urban landscape as part of its imaginary and historical reality. In Wang's own words, "Moving house cuts apart my space, dividing the space of my life into pieces."① The imprint of gender is vividly expressed in descriptions of the domestic domain. Wang's stories about families describe a vivid difference between spaces belonging to boys and those belonging to girls. Brothers and sisters have distinct rights within the family space. Behind these descriptions we also see signals of class status. These divisions are based on Wang's analysis of people's relationship to the means of production. Thus, in addition to gendered space, her writings also delimit spaces where productive activity takes place. While the former is linked to issues of sexuality, the latter pertains to labor and social values.

Wang's representations of space involve two turns. One goes from everyday life to a place of the spirit, and the other from materiality to production. As Gang Yue has observed, the "embodied space" (Yue's term) in *The Song of Everlasting Sorrow* is more for cooking and eating

---

① Howard Y. F. Choy, "From Pacific Ocean to Gobi Desert: Wang Anyi's Migratory Mythology," In Choy, *Remapping the Past: Fictions of History in Deng's China*, 1979 - 1997. Leiden: Brill, 2008, p. 73.

activities. The stove in Wang Qiyao's home-clinic is awarming and cooking utility and much more important to story than the incidentally mentioned alcohol burner used to disinfect needles in Wang's daily work as a home-based nurse. "Evening chats around the stove" are clearly central to the daily life of Wang Qiyao and her friends.①In this sense, the space represented in *The Song of Everlasting Sorrow* can be understood as a celebration of everyday life and materiality. Even Mr. Cheng's dark room is this type of space (everyday life and space of materiality), because it materializes beauty. In *The Age of Enlightenment*, Wang frames domestic spaces in people's homes as places where intellectual discussions occur. Here mundane material life is replaced by cultural and intellectual life. In *Fu Ping*, *Peach Trees in Full Blossom*, and *Scent of Heaven*, places where everyday life happens are turned into sites of production, which in turn become conflated with sexuality.

Here I would like to focus on the ambiguity of spaces of production and sexuality, and the conflicts between them. For example, in *Peach Trees in Full Blossom*, Wang presents sexuality in connection with various places and links it to productivity. Wang takes many paragraphs in different chapters to closely describe the heroine Yu Xiaoqiu's body. Besides the initial enumeration of Yu's hyper-feminine features, her body is described in terms of natural imagery such as flowers and fruit. At the same time, these descriptions of Yu's body always accompany some account of her production activities. As she highlights Yu Xiaoqiu's body, Wang focuses on how she works in a community factory. During the years as she grew from a girl into a woman, her body functioned a barrier to the growth of her feminine self-identity. This experience is very common for women of Yu Xiaoqiu's age. During the socialist period, when state ideology and

---

① Wang Anyi, *The Song of Everlasting Sorrow*, translated by Michael Berry and Susan Chan Egan. New York: Columbia University Press, 2008, pp. 162, 192 – 193.

bureaucracy together minimized women's feminine consciousness, their bodies often became the sources of their self-questioning. They felt ashamed as they witnessed the growth and changes in their bodies. Conflict and tensions between Yu's body and her environment—the space of production—arise.

There is a kind of masculine gaze in the space of production (the workplace), which turns Yu's body into a passive entity. Still, Yu is a worker, a laborer. From the perspective of this identity, the conflict between sexuality and her social nature is only sharpened. But the previous conflict between sexuality and revolutionary reality, which prevents her from participating in revolutionary dances, resolves into a conflict between sexuality and productivity. The former conflict is more ideologically oriented, while the latter is more neutral. While the masculine gaze of the male workers turns Yu's body into an object to be looked at, they also discover her charm. Her beauty, which was considered too sexual for revolutionary dances, is suitable in the community factory. In this sense, the working environment adds something to her sexuality, which also turns the space of production into the space of sexuality.

But the appreciation of the male workers, like all the criticisms in the past, kindles Yu's self-doubt. As her mind develops, she questions her own body. In other words, conflict arises between the spaces of production and sexuality. The latter is controlled by the male gaze in Chinese society, and Yu's self-doubt flourishes under that gaze and from feelings of shame in the process of discovering her body. The discourse of sexuality itself is ambiguous, just as the beauty of Yu's body is not a refined type of beauty, but earthy.

Production and Labor: The Margin and the Centre of the City

Wang sites production and labor in line with the spatial divisions and practices of the city, which frame Shanghai as margin and urban center. Wang Anyi shifts her geographical focus from the commercial center of Shanghai to its marginal areas in her writings after *The Everlasting Sorrow*. This geographical move is also a cultural and political move, which reveal her ongoing reflections about the commercialization of society. As she becomes concerned with the relationship between the center and margins of the city, Wang brings a sharper focus to its margins. *Fu Ping* provides a good example of this and marked a turning point in Wang's treatment of the dialectics between the center and the margin. [①]A girl from the countryside, Fu Ping is sent to Shanghai into an arranged marriage. The drive behind this move was materialistic: living in Shanghai would mean a better and more stable life for a country girl. Wang's Fu Ping is a woman searching for her own true subjectivity, and when she eventually finds Meijia Bridge, a marginal area of Shanghai, she discovers many local people who work hard to make a living. Thus, she finds not only a space of production or space of labor, but also labor itself. There, bodies are shaped into bodies that are the subjects of productions. They are productive beings instead of being the object of some external gaze or source of entertainment. In this sense, it is not Meijia Bridge, the physical place, but labor taking place there that becomes the basis of utopia.

The discovery of labor is linked to Wang's turn to the rural elements

① As Wang Xiaoming noted in his essay "From Huaihai Road to Meijia Bridge", in *Literary Review* (Wenxue pinglun), 2002, No. 3.

and marginal areas of Shanghai, as well as her search for the origins of the city. If for Eileen Chang turning to "ancient China" and "rural China" means turning to the vital sources of China's cultural strength,① Wang Anyi provides a different access to "rural China" with her exploration of the rural within the city. Once she had displayed the splendid surface of the metropolis (as a writer whose work epitomized "Shanghai Romance"), Wang turned to uncovering its origins and the legend of its prehistory.

In her important novel, *Records and Fiction* (*Jishi he xugou*), the city is described as a new beginning after chaos:

> The streets of the city bring a world of chaos into focus. They divide the surface while the buildings organize the space. After this, everything has its own name. ②

Here, the emergence of the city is a process of naming and re-naming. Unlike Eileen Chang, who attempts to recall the spirit of ancient China from the soil of its metropolis, Wang Anyi goes at the rescue of history from a different angle. In *Records and Fiction*, Wang endeavors to find traces of "family myth" in Shanghai, which means, to discover the legend, the genealogical memory of this modern city. Generally speaking, the very notion of "family myth" is alien to a metropolis such as Shanghai. So when it encounters the city, it loses its gravity:

> To tell the truth, in Shanghai few households have preserved their family myths, and another few have none at all. More cases fall in

---

① Please refer to my paper "The Discovery of Ancient China in Modern Shanghai: Eileen Chang's Reflections on Chinese Civilization and Shanghai Modernity".

② Wang Anyi, *Records and Fiction* (*Jishi he xugou*). Beijing: People's Literature Press, 2009, p. 48.

> between, meaning the family myth appears in a twisted form. It takes on a certain absurd air, just like a farce. ①

This being the case, the sublimity that family myths usually preserve around human experience is replaced by a kind of aesthetics of everyday life:

> Beautiful images such as fish and tree have been replaced by trivial and vulgar things; the disappearance of myth is accompanied by a taste for social news. ②

From legend to social news, the disenchantment of family myth is, in Walter Benjamin's sense, one part of the urban experience.

The tracing of family myth means tracing back to the origins of the city. Wang Anyi says:

> The origin is important to us because it enables us to see at least the truth of one side, and this prevents us from being absolutely lost. "Being lost" is the most common feeling of people in Shanghai. ③

Such tracing back is both temporal and spatial. In general, the prehistory of socialist Shanghai should mean its colonial period, but Wang Anyi is more interested in the prehistory of Shanghai before it became a metropolis; she is looking for the decisive power beneath its prosperity. Thus, in her later novels, Wang engages herself in re-mapping

---

① Wang Anyi, *Records and Fiction* (*Jishi he xugou*). Beijing: People's Literature Press, 2009, p. 48.

② Ibid., p. 48.

③ Ibid., p. 49.

the urban landscape. Rather than focusing on the prosperous face of Shanghai, she looks to its margins, its voids, the rural part of the metropolis. In *Records and Fiction*, she records how a group young suburban people think about the city:

> They refer to downtown as "Shanghai". They say: I went to Shanghai yesterday. It implies that the city's margins where they live cannot be understood as "Shanghai" ...They constitute a county-like community at the edge of Shanghai. This community allows them to keep a distance from Shanghai, the city. ①

Their existence at the margins defines the space of the metropolis. We may say that it is then the country that "names" the city.

Wang Anyi also wants to discover the spirit of the margin. In another novel *Little Sister* (*Mei Tou*), Wang lets two boys bring the reader to a wide square in the city. As all of the usual noise recedes, the vastness and sublimity of urban space are revealed:

> ...The sky above People's Square is unusually vast, which makes their hearts soar.
>
> Their speaking voices are also dispersed and float above their heads. They are moved by the sheer vastness. Kids living in the city center really do not know what is "huge" and what is "distant", because they have never freed their line of sight. ②

---

① Wang Anyi, *Records and Fiction* (*Jishi he xugou*). Beijing: People's Literature Press, 2009, p. 218.

② Wang Anyi, *Litter Sister* (*Mei tou*). Haikou: Nanhai Publishing House, 2000, pp. 52 – 54.

By re-mapping the metropolis-country structure, Wang Anyi discovers the void areas in the city, which leads to a new realm of the urban experience.

Wang Anyi is also interested in things that lie behind the city's prosperity, such as coal, which fuels much of the labor and production within the city. [1]In an essay titled "Tired Urban Dwellers", she says: "All Shanghainese live in an abstract world filled with symbols." Here, "symbols" is her word for the hidden constructive elements of the city[2]. While Eileen Chang finds the last hope for rescuing civilization in the wasteland, Wang discovers the power of the soil that lies beneath the city's prosperity. She calls it the foundation of Shanghai. The strength of the soil cannot be found in the city center, but is always hidden at its edges. In another essay, "The Sky of the Master" (*Zhuren de tiankong*), Wang invites the reader to appreciate the strength at the city from its margin:

> Sometimes, when you walk at the edge of the city, you suddenly feel that the sky has become wider. Tall buildings disappear; the prosperous downtown is replaced by wide roads. The scenes are pushed back far away into the distance. [3]

Wang sees the emptiness of the margin as constituting the real heart of this flashy city. Moreover, the margins are associated with labor and it is the labor that is the real master here. Thus, she concludes:

> These are the sound and scene at the margins of Shanghai, well

---

① Wang Anyi, "Pieces about Coal" (*Guanyu meitan de pianduan*), in Wang Anyi, *Soliloquies* (*Duyu*). Taibei: Maitian chuban youxian gongsi, 2000, p. 69.

② Wang Anyi "Tired Urban People" (*Pibei de dushi ren*), in *Close to the Beginning of a Century* (*Jiejin Shijichu*). Hangzhou: Zhejiang wenyi chubanshe, 1998, p. 44.

③ Wang Anyi, "The sky of the Master" (*Zhuren de tiankong*), in Wang Anyi, *Searching for Shanghai* (*Xunzhao shanghai*). Shanghai: Xuelin chubanshe, 2001, pp. 122 – 123.

> away from the din of the metropolis. They seem unconnected to the urban landscape and thus have a lonely aspect. However, here are the true foundations of Shanghai. They are at the core of Shanghai's splendor; without them, all that brilliance is superficial. ... People always say that Shanghai is romantic, but that is only its outward appearance. Its bones are made of steel and concrete. People always exaggerate Shanghai's entertainments, but who knows its labor? ...It is labor that is the true drama of Shanghai and its true master. Thus, the geographic margins are in fact the city's core, from where all dramatic causes begin and end. All the splendor and prosperity in the central areas of Shanghai are somehow not real; all the people and stories (there) are superficial.... but under the vast sky, there is the real life, the laboring life and survival of the masters of the city. ①

Thus, if in temporal terms Eileen Chang pushes the prehistory of the city into its primitive status, then Wang Anyi spatially traces its origin to its margin. If what Eileen Chang emphasizes is human beings' strong will which confronts the wasteland, then what interests Wang Anyi is the hard, heavy "labor" beneath the floating dust of the city.

Discovering the Labor Beneath

In his "Narratives on Labor or the Utopia of Labor," Cai Xiang examines the development of the concept "labor" (*laodong*) in twentieth-century China. He introduces how Communist pioneers such as Li Dazhao Sinicized the Marxist notion of labor, and how Mao Zedong developed

---

① Wang Anyi, "The sky of the Master" (*Zhuren de tiankong*), in Wang Anyi, *Searching for Shanghai* (*Xunzhao shanghai*). Shanghai: Xuelin chubanshe, 2001, pp. 122 – 123.

from the worship of physical labor to seeing the peasants and workers as the major force of revolution. Cai indicates that labor was "one of the most important notions in the left-wing thought of twentieth-century China".① "Combined with the concept of the proletariat, it opens up a kind of politics that not only belongs to one nation, but also belongs to the world: a regime's imagined and actual practice (of politics)."② This reconstructed notion of labor confirms the significance of workers as "political and economic, emotional and ethical" subjects and thus requires the establishment of a new *Lebenwelt* (lifeworld).③

In his analysis of Zhao Shuli's "The Land" (*Diban*), Cai Xiang emphasizes the author's treatment of the relationship between land and labor. He points to the liberation of the lower levels of society not only as occurring "at the political and economic levels," but also as including "the dignity of the lower classes".④ In "Land," such dignity is confirmed "in its discussion of the subjectivity of labor".⑤ The lower class's claiming dignity further "establishes the legitimacy of labor".⑥ By introducing discussion on whether land or labor creates food, Zhao Shuli touches upon crucial issues concerning the social transformation of China: proprietorship and its transfer, the distribution of land, and relations between the landlord class and the tenant class.

If we place Wang Anyi's writings on labor in the genealogy of the contemporary Chinese literature, we note the following traits. First, Wang

---

① Cai Xiang, ""Narratives of Labor or Labor Utopias" (Laodong huozhe laodong wutuobang de xushu), in his book *Revolution and Its Narratives: China's Socialist Literary and Cultural Imaginaries, 1949 – 1966* (*Geming/Xushu*). Beijing: Peking University Press, 2010, pp. 136 – 137.

② Ibid., p. 137.

③ Ibid.

④ Ibid., p. 142.

⑤ Ibid.

⑥ Ibid.

inherits the legacy of the left-wing thought and literature; second, she sites labor in the dialectic between city and country; third, she injects labor into the urban writings of contemporary China. What can we learn from a comparison of Zhao Shuli, Eileen Chang, Yan Geling, and Wang Anyi's treatment of labor? In "Land", Zhao Shuli creates an intertextual discourse of labor by introducing a discussion of the relations between land and labor; in *The Rice-Sprout Song*, Eileen Chang points to the uselessness of labor to resist hunger and death. Yan Geling dismisses the crucial issues such as proprietorship, exploitation, and inequality between landlord and tenant by creating an image of landlords as laborers. By constructing a feminine space of labor such as that in the Tianxiang Garden in *Scent of Heaven*, Wang Anyi combines labor and feminism. In this regard, Wang and Yan share certain similarities, yet also differ in some respects. First, both are good at depicting earth mothers as I argued above. Second, the earth mothers in Wang and Yan's writings are always good laborers. Third, while Yan does not engage withan imaginary division of urban space in her texts, Wang links labor and production to her remapping of the urban margins and center. If the margin constitutes the real center of the city for Wang Anyi, and labor is the real bedrock of the margin, then labor can be called the true soul of the metropolis. In "The Sky of the Master", where Wang claims labor as the true basis of the city, she implies that it is not only an element in the circulation of capital, money, and products, but in fact has its own subjectivity. This is to say, when she calls "labor" the master of the city, she cuts the link between labor and the laborer. In other words, labor becomes an abstract concept. It becomes a value that is unchangeable. Here, we can see how Wang tries to resist neo-ideologies by mapping out "labor" beneath the city's surface. But labor itself is, significantly, not a pure concept. It is not self-evident or self-sufficient but always engulfed in the class structure and social relationships. The questions around labor include: Who buys it? Who pays for it? In the process of using it, what is produced and what is thrown away? What is the process by which "labor" is produced and reproduced? When Wang Anyi makes a clear distinction between "laboring" Shanghai and luxurious Shanghai, she ignores the exchange and flow of the power between these two. In other words, luxurious Shanghai and the working-class Shanghai are not two juxtaposed things, but two ends of one contradiction. In Wang's recent works, this notion of labor has become a new myth that is put into play to resist the sweeping commodification of Chinese society.

Production and Femininity

If *Records and Fiction* tries to recover the legend of Shanghai, then in *Scent of Heaven* (*Tianxiang*), Wang traces Shanghai to its prehistory—the origins of secularism, consumption, and capitalism. This novel traces commercial society back to the late Ming. The Tianxiang Garden is the private garden of a rich Shanghai family. It is named Tianxiang because of the peach trees in the garden. If the title of the novel *Peach Tree in Full Blossom* suggests the full potential of production (in terms of both bodily reproduction and labor/production), then the name Tianxiang (scent of heaven) not only points to rich materiality in the wealth of this family, but also suggests the productivity that embodies the potential to rescue the family in it decline. The Tianxiang Garden is supposed to be exclusive, but Wang Anyi uses the activities of production to link the inner and the outer. She locates the sprouting of commercialism and capitalism in the late Ming in this Garden by having the residents of the Tianxiang Garden (the upper class) set up a mock market that includes various types of shops such as bookstores, pharmacies, and even a butcher shop. The butcher shop is especially critical to giving this event its commercial flavor. While the market reveals the Tianxiang Garden as a place where commerce can take place, a space for consumers, the author also presents another aspect of the garden, as a place for laborers.

The Tianxiang Garden is gradually transformed from a space that displays a luxurious and delicate lifestyle to a space of production, where women get together to make embroidered items. The "pavilion of embroidery" (*xiuge*) is a place where women can gather to rescue themselves from their broken relationship with men. One character, Xiao Chou, puts all her energy into her embroidery work there after she stops communicating with her husband because he has taken in a concubine.[①] Later, when Xiao Chou's nephew A Qian leaves home without any notice, leaving his wife Xi Zhao behind at home, Xi Zhao also tries to save herself by going to the embroidery pavilion to produce embroidered scenic works. At a deeper level, as the family continues to decline, it is these women as laborers and producers who take charge of saving their household. In this sense, the Tianxiang Garden becomes a kind of feminine utopia, a utopia of production, capable of resisting the decline of history.

In *Scent of Heaven*, Wang Anyi always describes the physical beauty (external features) and spiritual superiority (internal features) of women in relation to production and productivity. For example, Xiao Chou's husband was first attracted by the daughter of the Min family when she was doing embroidery, and decided to marry her as a concubine. Similarly, the spiritual superiority of Xiao Chou and Xi Zhao is portrayed as an unusual feminine quality that is expressed in their embroidery products. Once sexuality and femininity are framed in terms of production, female friendship and mutual support, which are based on their common engagement in the art of embroidery, eclipse relations between men and women. In the Shen family, it was the women who gradually became

---

① Wang Anyi, *Scent of Heaven* (*Tianxiang*). Beijing: People's Literature Press, 2011, p. 237.

carriers of the family's burdens, while the man only knew how to spend money. With an emphasis on womanliness and the absence of manliness, production becomes a domain of femininity.

The uniqueness of Wang Anyi's construction of a feminine utopia based on labor can be clearly seen if we compare her treatment with that by the Taiwan novelist Zhu Tianwen, who also engages in imagining women as the final carriers of history. In her story "Fin de Siècle Splendor" (*Shijimo de huali*), Zhu's female protagonist Mia spends most of her time producing splendid papers. These not only fill Mia's life, but also flow across the boundary of the text. As a metaphor, the abundance and splendor of these papers are the last remains in the ruins of history. At the end of "Fin de Siècle Splendor," Zhu devotes several passages to describing the delicacy of the colorful papers, but only uses a single sentence to introduce the possibility that Mia will become an artisan able to make a living by creating these papers. Furthermore, she does not stress the collective dimension of labor in a community. Zhu's individualistic treatment of the relationship between human beings and the material world takes an individualistic view of the end of history. Although Zhu points out that a woman like Mia can recreate a world based on her memories of "smells and colors" after the "world men have built with theories and systems" collapses, the subjectivity of women in fact is subverted by material.① Material has become the subject and obtains its own subjectivity. Material eclipses the human being as the latter loses its subjectivity. History in Zhu's writing is destructive and limited to individualistic survival. Wang Anyi, by contrast, always emphasizes the subjectivity of laborers as the carriers of history. Without the collective dimension of labor and laborers, Zhu Tianwen's feminine space is filled with feminine details, but lacks the

① Zhu Tianwen, "Fin de Siècle Splendor", translated by Eva Hung, in *The Columbia Anthology of Modern Chinese Literature*. New York: Columbian University Press, 2007, pp. 388 – 402.

organic relation between femininity and production in the larger context of society. It is exclusive and only opens to pessimistic individuals like Mia. In other words, Zhu's feminine space is static and closed, based on historical nihilism, while Wang Anyi conveys movement by calling special attention to labor and production, both of which rely on action. Wang's representation of these occurs at a collective level and in a larger context of the comprehensive transformation of a nation or a society in the world-history sense: the evolution of a classical society towards a commercial one (*Scent of Heaven*), the Socialist reconstruction of society (*Fu Ping*, *Peach Trees in Full Blossom*), or the transition from a socialist state towards a market economy (*Grow Red Water Chestnut Above and Lotus Root Below* [*Shang zhong hongling xia zhong ou*]). The space of production in Wang's writings always flows. Production can be extended from an interiorplace such as the Tianxiang Garden to the outside world. In *Scent of Heaven*, long after the mock market has taken place, a real shop figures productively in the story: A Fang's Tofu Shop in town. The success of this shop prompts A Fang to give up his original plan to become a governmental official by sitting for the civil service examination, a development that signals the rise of commercialism in the late Ming.

Moreover, Wang Anyi also stresses the signification of production by inviting characters in the story to express their opinions on labor, production, and productivity, as when Xiao Chou criticizes Xi Zhao for producing embroidered pictures only for their aesthetics but not for use. Hence, the emphasis on production is intertwined with the value of utility and the secular, mundane aspects of urban life.

Conclusion

Wang Anyi's work is special in the spectrum of contemporary Chinese literature because of her constant engagement with the changing social landscape in various periods. While she is not a pioneer feminist embracing the edge-cutting theories, Wang's literary practice shows that she is a moderate feminist writer who not only links women and nature but also rethinks their capacity for production and reproduction. She is not against the social norms or customs, but rather incorporates the values recognized as female by society into her construction of ideal women as producers and laborers. Her depictions of female experience move from the image of the Shanghai beauty to that of the earth mother. The typical earth mother always commands a feminine consciousness and identity without undergoing a self-conscious search. In other words, she obtains a kind of unconscious feminine/feminist consciousness. The transition in Wang's work from Shanghai beauty to earth mother parallels the retreat of sexuality and rise of productivity in her representation of women, both of which are intertwined with her redefinition of true femininity as the strength of soft power that can eclipse masculinity and rescue women themselves and history. Wang's emphasis on women's capacity to produce and reproduce leads to her construction of a poetic space that is not only feminine in the traditional sense, but also a space of labor, where production becomes a feminine utopia. Her discovery of the poetic space of labor is integrated with her remapping of Shanghai and the relationship between margin and center in her texts. The poetic space of labor and production Wang constructs sits either at the margins or behind the curtain of splendor that is the metropolis. In this way, she successfully turns Shanghai from a realm of entertainments to a domain of productivity. And by this she has achieved something unique among the urban writings of contemporary China.